FT

DATE			
68X	6/11 ✓ 3/12		
74X	3/12	6/14	

FAIRY TALE SHELF PO
1495

83 ⑧⑧
⑧④ ⑧⑨
⑧⑤
⑧⑥
AUG   1982

© THE BAKER & TAYLOR CO.

FAIRY TALES *of the* BROTHERS GRIMM

Illustrated by
KAY NIELSEN

FAIRY TALES *of the* BROTHERS GRIMM

Illustrated by
KAY NIELSEN
With an Introduction by Bryan Holme

A Studio Book
The Metropolitan Museum of Art
and
The Viking Press · New York

Introduction Copyright in all Countries of the International
Copyright Union by Viking Penguin Inc., 1979

First published in 1979 by The Viking Press/A Studio Book
625 Madison Avenue, New York, N.Y. 10022
Published simultaneously in Canada by
Penguin Books Canada Limited

Library of Congress Cataloging in Publication Data
Grimm, Jakob Ludwig Karl, 1785–1863.
Fairy tales of the Brothers Grimm.
(A Studio book)
Translation of 12 of the Kinder- und Hausmärchen,
with the illustrations originally published in Fleur-de-Neige
et d'autres contes de Grimm, Paris, 1925.

Summary: Included among the 12 fairy tales in
this facsimile edition are "Snowdrop," "Hansel and Gretel,"
"Cherry, or the Frog Bride," and "The Goose Girl."

1. Fairy tales, German.   [1. Fairy tales.
2. Folklore—Germany]   I. Grimm, Wilhelm Karl,
1786–1859, joint author.   II. Nielsen, Kay Rasmus,
1886–1957.   III. Title.
PZ8.G882Fai   1979b   398.2'1'0943   79-12945

ISBN 0-670-30565-0
Printed in Japan by Dai Nippon Printing Co., Ltd., Tokyo
Set in Baskerville

CONTENTS

INTRODUCTION

"Snowdrop," "The Six Swans," "Hansel and Gretel," and all the other "household" stories the pioneering Grimm brothers collected in the early nineteenth century remain well remembered and just as well loved by children today, surely, as in the days when they were first published.

Almost but perhaps not quite so famous as the tales themselves is the story behind them: how the two German brothers, Jacob and Wilhelm Grimm, remembering the stories they had listened to, wide-eyed, as orphans at their guardian aunt's house in Hesse, decided not only to write these down but to comb the neighboring towns, villages, hamlets, and remote country cottages for old storytellers who were still recounting tales that had been handed down orally in their families for generations. Some of the household stories the Grimms collected were variations of the fairy tales they already knew; others were different.

In 1812, when the brothers finished selecting and editing the best of their collection, they discovered they had enough tales to fill not just one volume but two. No sooner had these been published in Germany than the fame of the Grimm brothers spread like wildfire across Europe. For some reason, however, the English-speaking world had to wait eleven long years for the first volume of *German Household Stories*—translated by Edgar Taylor and illustrated by George Cruikshank—to be published, and another two years for the second.

Part of the great excitement over the English edition in 1823 was the fact that it had been illustrated—a milestone in publishing, which marked it as "the first picture book for children—in the modern sense." It was also a turning point for George Cruikshank, hitherto little known, who was to go on to become the foremost—and most prolific—English illustrator of his time.

The 1820s and Cruikshank's illustrations for Grimm's fairy

tales can be said to represent the very beginning of the so-called Golden Age of illustration. By something of a coincidence, the 1920s and Kay Nielsen's illustrations for Grimm's fairy tales—those that appear in this book—represent the close of that glittering age after it had lasted for almost exactly one hundred years.

Meanwhile, a high point had been reached when selective parents had come to expect that a volume of fairy tales would not only be illustrated by a major artist like Arthur Rackham, Edmund Dulac, or Kay Nielsen but would be well printed in full color and handsomely bound—in effect, a book that was likely to afford them as much pleasure as it would the children, who were, of course, their excuse for investing in the book in the first place.

Were it possible to place side by side four of the best illustrated editions of Grimm's fairy tales published during the Golden Age—namely, the two that were illustrated in black and white—by George Cruikshank in 1824 and by Walter Crane in 1886—and the two illustrated in color—by Arthur Rackham in 1909 and by Kay Nielsen in 1925—quickly and clearly we would see what changing fashions did to the style of illustration during the long course of the Golden Age and what a dramatic difference the perfection of the color-reproduction process was to make after the turn of the century.

Kay Rasmus Nielsen, who was born in Copenhagen in 1886, became passionately interested in art, literature, and the theater while he was still in his teens. This was natural enough, for both his actor father, Martinius Nielsen, who later became the Director of the Royal Danish Theater, and his mother, the actress Oda Larssen, were constantly "at home" to writers, designers, actors, and every imaginable other talent connected with their glamorous profession.

In 1904, at the age of eighteen and already under the influence of the English artist Aubrey Beardsley and the Art Deco movement in general, Kay Nielsen left Copenhagen to study at the Académie Julienne in Paris. Seven years later he left Paris for London and in

1912 was holding his first exhibition, a series of black-and-white illustrations for a proposed publication, *The Book of Death,* at the Dowdeswell Galleries in New Bond Street. The drawings were viewed by the London publishers Hodder and Stoughton, who, to his disappointment, were unable "quite" to visualize a book developing out of them but who nevertheless did recognize in Nielsen precisely the kind of genius they were looking for to illustrate a fancy edition of fairy tales they had in mind.

This resulted in the first of the four great fairy-tale books that have earned Nielsen his special niche in history. *In Powder and Crinoline,* a book of old fairy tales retold by Sir Arthur Quiller-Couch, was published in 1913, and an exhibition of the twenty-four original Nielsen watercolors was held at the small but prestigious Leicester Galleries. A similar show was arranged in 1914 to coincide with the publication of Nielsen's second and greater masterpiece, *East of the Sun and West of the Moon; Old Tales from the North,* with texts by Asbjömsen and Moe.

The year 1914 was, of course, one of the saddest in European history. In England and on most of the Continent the outbreak of World War I called a halt to cultural endeavors on all fronts. Those who weren't fighting, or dying, spent the best part of their energies working for those who were. Thus the all-too-short chain of Kay Nielsen's books was broken, and it was to remain broken for a full six years after the war ended while Nielsen became increasingly involved in mounting extravagantly beautiful productions of *Aladdin, Scaramouche,* and other spectacles at the Danish State Theater in collaboration with the young actor-producer Johannes Poulsen.

When Nielsen finally returned to the world of books in 1924 with the illustrations for *Hans Andersen's Fairy Tales,* his brush had lost none of its magic touch. In the year following, he completed the twelve superb watercolors for the Grimm's tales that are to be found in the following pages. They are, perhaps, the best set of illustrations he ever did.

The English-language edition of this last great work by Nielsen was entitled *Hansel and Gretel; Stories from the Brothers Grimm.* In France the publishers, L'Edition d'Art, called the same book *Fleur-de-Neige* because "Snow White" or "Snowdrop" sounded more melodious in French and, they thought, was a more appealing story anyway.

The texts that follow are taken from the first English edition, the color plates are from both the English and French first editions, and the exquisite chapter-head decorations and ornamental letters, executed in the Nielsen style by Pierre Courtois, are from the French edition.

Kay Nielsen's last book, *Red Magic; a Collection of the World's Best Fairy Tales from All Countries,* edited by Romer Wilson, was a smaller and an otherwise less impressive work than his earlier books. Published in 1930, five years after Nielsen had illustrated Grimm, and one year after the Wall Street crash, this work seemed sadly to emphasize the fact that both the taste and the economy of the world had changed by then and that the final curtain had been rung down on the Golden Age of illustration.

Acknowledging this fact, or trying to, Kay Nielsen and his young Danish wife, Ulla Pless-Schmidt, whom he had married in 1926, sailed for America and another world of make-believe, Hollywood, where he was to design motion-picture sets, take walk-on parts in films, and paint an occasional mural, living meanwhile in comparative obscurity until he died in 1957.

Although Kay Nielsen was recognized by the few—or the comparative few—as one of the greatest illustrators in a hundred years, his was the typical case of the artist who had to wait to be discovered by the world at large long after he had left it. To see Nielsen's name now in large print in art books and to see his exquisite and highly original illustrated books being rediscovered, republished, and loved the world over, makes it certain that, in this century at least, his name will be remembered.

Bryan Holme

9

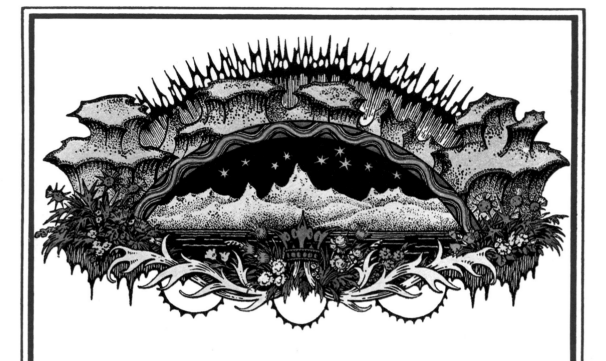

SNOWDROP

 LONG time ago, on a cold midwinter's day, when broad flakes of snow were falling all around, a certain Queen sat working at a window, the frame of which was made of fine black ebony, and as she was looking out at the snow, she pricked her finger, and three drops of blood fell on it. Then she gazed thoughtfully at the red drops that sprinkled the white snow, and said, "May my little daughter be as white as that snow, as red as the blood, and as black as the ebony window frame!" And so the little girl grew up; her skin was as white as snow, her cheeks as rosy as blood, and her hair as black as ebony, and she was called Snow-drop.

But this Queen died, and the King soon married another wife, who was very beautiful but so proud that she could not bear to think that anyone could surpass her. She had a magic looking glass, to which she used to go and gaze at herself in it, and say:

"Tell me, glass, tell me true!
Of all the ladies in the land,
Who is the fairest? Tell me who."

And the glass answered:

"Thou, Queen, art fairest in the land."

But Snowdrop grew more and more beautiful, and when she was seven years old she was as bright as the day and fairer than the Queen herself. Then one day the looking glass answered the Queen when she went to consult it as usual:

"Thou, Queen, may fair and beauteous be
But Snowdrop is lovelier far than thee!"

When she heard this, she turned pale with rage and envy and called to one of her servants and said, "Take Snowdrop away into the wide wood, so that I may never see her again." Then the servant led Snowdrop away, but his heart melted when she begged him to spare her life, and he said, "I will not hurt you, you pretty child." So he left her by herself, and though he thought it likely that the wild beasts would tear her to pieces, he felt as if a great weight had been lifted from his heart when he had made up his mind not to kill her, but to leave her to her fate.

Then poor Snowdrop wandered through the wood in great fear, and the wild beasts roared about her, but none did her any harm. In the evening she came to a little cottage and went inside to rest, for her little feet would carry her no farther. Everything was clean and neat in the cottage. A white cloth was spread on the table, and there were seven little plates with seven little loaves, and seven little glasses with wine in them, and knives and forks laid in order, and against the wall stood seven little beds. Then, as she was very hungry, she picked a little piece off each loaf, and drank a very little wine out of each glass, and after that she thought she would lie down and rest. She tried all the little beds. One was too long, and another was too short, till at last the seventh suited her, and there she lay down and went to sleep.

Presently in came the masters of the cottage, who were seven little dwarfs who lived in the midst of the mountains and dug and searched for gold. They lit their seven lamps and saw at once that all was not right. The first said, "Who has been sitting on my stool?" The second, "Who has been eating off my plate?" The third, "Who has been picking my bread?" The fourth, "Who has been meddling with my spoon?" The fifth, "Who has been handling my fork?" The sixth, "Who has been cutting with my knife?" The seventh, "Who has been drinking my wine?" Then the first looked around and said, "Who has been lying on my bed?" And the rest came running to him, and every one of them cried out that somebody had been on his bed. But the seventh saw Snowdrop and called all his brothers to come and see her, and they cried out with wonder and astonishment and brought their lamps to look at her and said, "Good heavens! What a lovely child she is!" And they were delighted to see her and were careful not to wake her, and the seventh dwarf slept an hour with each of the other dwarfs in turn, till the night was gone.

In the morning Snowdrop told them all her story, and they pitied her and said that if she would keep everything in order and cook and wash and knit and spin for them, she could stay where she was, and they would take good care of her. Then they went out all day long to their work, searching for gold and silver in the mountains, and Snowdrop stayed at home, and before they left they warned her and said, "The Queen will soon find out where you are, so take care and let no one in."

But the Queen, now that she thought Snowdrop was dead, believed that she was certainly the handsomest lady in the land, and she went to her looking glass and said:

"Tell me, glass, tell me true!
Of all the ladies in the land,
Who is the fairest? Tell me who."

And the glass answered:

"Thou, Queen, art the fairest in all this land,
But over the hills, in the greenwood shade,
Where the seven dwarfs their dwelling have made,
There Snowdrop is hiding her head, and she
Is lovelier far, O Queen, than thee!"

Then the Queen was very much alarmed, for she knew that the glass always spoke the truth, and she was sure that the servant had betrayed her. And she could not bear to think that anyone lived who was more beautiful than she was, so she disguised herself as an old peddler and went her way over the hills to the place where the dwarfs dwelt. Then she knocked at the door and cried, "Fine wares to sell!" Snowdrop looked out the window and said, "Good day, good woman. What have you to sell?" "Good wares, fine wares," said she, "laces and bobbins of all colors." Snowdrop thought, "I will let the old lady in—she seems to be a very good sort," and she ran down and unbolted the door. "Bless me!" said the old woman. "How badly your stays are laced! Let me lace them up with one of my nice new laces." Snowdrop did not dream of any mischief, so she stood up before the old woman, but the Queen set to work so nimbly and pulled the lace so tight that Snowdrop lost her breath and fell down as if she were dead. "There's an end of all your beauty," said the spiteful Queen, and went home.

In the evening the seven dwarfs returned. How grieved they were to see their faithful Snowdrop stretched on the floor motionless, as if she were quite dead. However, they lifted her up, and when they found what was the matter, they cut the lace, and in a little while she began to breathe and soon came to life again. Then they said, "The old woman was the Queen herself. Take care another time, and let no one in when we are away."

When the Queen got home, she went straight to her looking glass and spoke to it as usual, but to her great surprise it still said:

"Thou, Queen, art the fairest in all this land,
But over the hills, in the greenwood shade,
Where the seven dwarfs their dwelling have made,
There Snowdrop is hiding her head, and she
Is lovelier far, O Queen, than thee."

Then the blood ran cold in her heart with spite and malice now that she knew that Snowdrop still lived, and she dressed herself up again in a disguise, but very different from the one she'd worn before, and took with her a poisoned comb. When she reached the dwarfs' cottage, she knocked at the door and cried, "Fine wares to sell!" But Snowdrop said, "I dare not let anyone in." Then the Queen said, "Only look at my beautiful combs," and gave her the poisoned one. And it looked so pretty that she took it up and put it into her hair to try it, but the moment it touched her head the poison was so powerful that she fell down senseless. "There you may lie," said the Queen, and went her way. But by good luck the dwarfs returned very early that evening, and when they saw Snowdrop lying on the floor, they guessed what had happened, and soon found the poisoned comb. And when they took the comb out of her hair, she recovered and told them all that had happened, and they warned her once more not to open the door to anyone.

Meantime the Queen went home to her looking glass and trembled with rage when she received exactly the same answer as before, and she said, "Snowdrop shall die, if it costs me my life." So she went secretly into a chamber and prepared a poisoned apple; the outside looked very rosy and tempting, but whoever tasted it was sure to die. Then she dressed herself up as a peasant's wife and traveled over the hills to the dwarfs' cottage and knocked at the door, but Snowdrop put her head out of the window and said, "I dare not let anyone in, for the dwarfs have told me not to." "Do as you please," said the old woman, "but at any rate take this pretty apple—I will make you a present of it." "No," said Snowdrop, "I dare not take it." "You silly girl!" answered the Queen. "What are you afraid of? Do you think it is poisoned? Come! You eat one part, and I will eat the other." Now the apple was so prepared that one side was good, though the other side was poisoned. Then Snowdrop was very much tempted to taste the apple, for it looked exceedingly nice, and when she saw the old woman take a bite of it she could refrain no longer. But she had scarcely put the piece into her mouth when she fell down dead on the floor. "This time nothing will save you," said the Queen, and she went home to her glass, and at last it said:

"Thou, Queen, art the fairest of all the fair."

And then her envious heart was glad, and as happy as such a heart could be.

When evening came, and the dwarfs returned home, they found Snowdrop lying on the floor; no breath passed her lips, and they were afraid that she was dead. They lifted her and combed her hair and washed her face with wine and water, but all was in vain, for the little girl seemed quite dead. So they laid her down upon a bier, and all seven watched and bewailed her for three whole days, and then they proposed to bury her. But her cheeks were still rosy, and her face looked just as it had while she was alive, so they said, "We will never bury her in the cold ground." And they made a coffin of glass, so they might still look at her, and they wrote her name on it in golden letters, and that she was a King's daughter. And the coffin was placed upon the hill, and one of the dwarfs always sat by it and watched. And the birds came, too, and

bemoaned Snowdrop. First of all came an owl, and then a raven, but at last came a dove.

And thus Snowdrop lay for a long, long time, and still looked only as though she were asleep, for she was even now as white as snow, and as red as blood, and as black as ebony. At last a Prince came and called at the dwarfs' house, and he saw Snowdrop and read what was written in golden letters. Then he offered the dwarfs money and earnestly pleaded with them to let him take her away, but they said, "We will not part with her for all the gold in the world." At last, however, they had pity on him and gave him the coffin, but the moment he lifted it up to carry it home with him, the piece of apple fell from between her lips, and Snowdrop awoke and said, "Where am I?" And the Prince answered, "You are safe with me." Then he told her all that had happened and said, "I love you better than all the world. Come with me to my father's palace, and you shall be my wife." And Snowdrop consented and went home with the Prince, and everything was prepared with great pomp and splendor for their wedding.

To the feast was invited, among the rest, Snowdrop's old enemy, the Queen, and as she was dressing herself in fine rich clothes, she looked in the glass, and said:

"Tell me, glass, tell me true!
Of all the ladies in the land,
Who is the fairest? Tell me who."

And the glass answered:

"Thou, lady, art loveliest here, *I ween,*
But lovelier far is the new-made Queen."

When she heard this, she was filled with rage, but her envy and curiosity were so great that she could not help setting out to see the bride. And when she arrived and saw that it was no other than Snowdrop, who, as she thought, had been dead a long while, she choked with fury and fell ill and died, but Snowdrop and the Prince lived and reigned happily over that land many, many years.

18

HANSEL AND GRETEL

IN a cottage near a large wood there once dwelt a poor woodcutter with his wife and two children by his former marriage—a little boy called Hansel and a girl named Gretel. The woodcutter had little enough to break or bite, and once, when there was a great famine in the land, he could not procure even his daily bread, and as he lay thinking in his bed one evening, tossing and turning with worry, he sighed and said to his wife, "What will become of us? How can we feed our children when we have no more than we can eat ourselves?"

"Listen to me, my husband," she answered. "We will lead them away, quite early in the morning, into the thickest part of the wood, and there make them a fire and give them each a little piece of bread. Then we will go to our work and leave them alone, so they will not find the way home again, and we will be freed from them." "No, Wife," he replied. "That I can never do. How can you think of leaving my children all alone in the wood, for the wild beasts will soon come and tear them to pieces?"

"Oh, you simpleton!" said she. "Then we must all four die of hunger—you had better make coffins for us." But she gave him no peace till he consented, saying, "Ah, but I shall regret the poor children."

The two children, however, had been so hungry that they could not sleep, and so they had overheard what the stepmother said to their father. Gretel wept bitterly and said to Hansel, "What will become of us?" "Be quiet, Gretel," said he. "Do not cry—I will soon help you." And as soon as their parents had fallen asleep, he got up, put on his coat, and, unbarring the back door, slipped out. The moon shone brightly, and the white pebbles that lay before the door seemed like silver pieces, they glittered so brightly. Hansel stooped and put as many into his pocket as it would hold. Then he went back to the house and said to Gretel, "Be comforted, dear sister, and sleep in peace. God will not forsake us." And so saying, he went to bed again.

The next morning, before the sun rose, the wife awoke the two children. "Get up, you lazy things! We are going into the forest to chop wood." Then she gave them each a piece of bread, saying, "There is something for your dinner. Do not eat it right away, for you will get nothing else." Gretel took the bread in her apron, for Hansel's pocket was full of pebbles, and so they all set out on their way. When they had gone a little distance, Hansel stopped and looked back at the house. He repeated this several times, till his father said, "Hansel, what are you looking at, and why do you lag behind? Take care and keep walking."

"Ah, Father," said Hansel, "I am looking at my white cat sitting on the roof of the house and trying to say good-bye." "You simpleton!'' said the wife. ''That is not a cat—it is only the sun shining on the white chimney.'' But in reality Hansel was not looking at a cat; every time he stopped, he dropped a pebble out of his pocket on the path.

When they came to the middle of the forest, the father told the children to collect wood, and he would make them a fire so they would not be cold. So Hansel and Gretel gathered together quite a little mountain of twigs. Then they set fire to them, and as the flames burned up high, the wife said, ''Now, you children, lie down near the fire and rest yourselves while we go into the forest and chop wood. When we are ready, I will come and get you.''

Hansel and Gretel sat down by the fire, and when it was noon, they ate their pieces of bread, and because they could hear the blows of an ax they thought their father was near. But it was not an ax; it was a branch he had bound to a dead tree so it would be blown to and fro by the wind. They waited so long that at last their eyes closed from weariness and they fell fast asleep. When they awoke, it was quite dark, and Gretel began to cry, ''How will we get out of the wood?'' But Hansel tried to comfort her by saying, ''Wait a little while till the moon rises, and then we will quickly find the way.'' The moon soon shone forth, and Hansel, taking his sister's hand, followed the pebbles, which glittered like new-minted silver pieces and showed them the path. All night long they walked on, and as day broke they came to their father's house. They knocked at the door, and when the wife opened it and saw Hansel and Gretel, she exclaimed, ''You wicked children! Why did you sleep so long in the wood? We thought you were never coming home again.'' But their father was very glad, for it had grieved his heart to leave them all alone.

Not long afterward there was again great scarcity in every corner of the land, and one night the children overheard their stepmother saying to their father, ''We have eaten everything. There is only half a loaf left, and then it will be all over for us. The children must be sent away. We will take them deeper into the wood, so they will not find their way out again. It is the only thing for us to do."

But her husband's heart was heavy, and he thought, "It would be better to share the last crust with the children." His wife, however, would listen to nothing he said, and scolded and reproached him without end.

He who says A must say B too, and he who consents the first time must also agree the second time.

The children, however, had heard the conversation as they lay awake, and as soon as the old people went to sleep, Hansel got up, intending to pick up some pebbles as before, but the wife had locked the door, so he could not get out. Nevertheless, he comforted Gretel, saying, "Don't cry, go to sleep. The good Lord will not forsake us."

Early in the morning the stepmother came and pulled them out of bed and gave them each a slice of bread, which was even smaller than the previous piece had been. On the way Hansel broke his piece of bread in his pocket and, stooping every now and then, dropped a crumb on the path. "Hansel, why do you stop and look around like that?" asked the father. "Keep on the path." "I am looking at my little dove," answered Hansel, "nodding good-bye to me." "Simpleton!" said the wife. "That is no dove—it's only the sun shining on the chimney." But Hansel still dropped crumbs as he went along.

The wife led the children deep into the wood, where they had never been before. There she made an immense fire and said to them, "Sit down here and rest, and when you feel tired you can sleep for a little while. We are going into the forest to chop wood, and in the evening, when we are ready, we will come and fetch you."

At noon Gretel shared her bread with Hansel, who had strewn his on the path. Then they went to sleep, but by evening no one had come to visit the poor children, and in the dark night they awoke, and Hansel comforted his sister by saying, "Wait, Gretel, till the moon comes out—then we shall see the crumbs of bread I have dropped, and they will show us the way home." The moon shone, and they got up, but they could not see any crumbs, for the thousands of birds which had been flying about in the woods and fields had picked them all up. Hansel kept saying to Gretel, "We will soon find the way," but they did not. They walked all night long and the next day, but still they did not come out of the wood, and they got so hungry, for they had nothing to eat but the berries they found on the bushes. Soon they got so tired that they could not drag themselves any farther, so they lay down under a tree and went to sleep.

It was now the third morning since they had left their father's house, and they still walked on, but they only got deeper and deeper into the forest, and Hansel knew that if help did not come very soon they would die of hunger. At noon they saw a beautiful snow-white bird sitting on a bough, which sang so sweetly that they stood still and listened to it. It soon stopped singing and, spreading its wings, flew off. They followed it until it arrived at a cottage, where the bird perched on the roof. When they went close to it, they saw that the cottage was made of bread and cakes, and the windowpanes were of clear sugar.

"We will go in here," said Hansel, "and have a glorious feast. I will eat a piece of the roof, and you can eat the window. Won't that be sweet?" Hansel reached up and broke off a piece of the roof in order to see how it tasted, while Gretel stepped up to the window and began to bite it.

Then a sweet voice called out from inside, "Tip-tap, tip-tap, who raps at my door?" and the children answered, "The wind, the wind, the child of heaven!" and they went on eating without interruption. Hansel thought the roof tasted very nice, and he tore off a great piece, while Gretel broke a large round windowpane and sat down quite contentedly to eat it. Just then the door opened and a very old woman, on crutches, came out.

Hansel and Gretel were so frightened that they let go what

they had in their hands, but the old woman, nodding her head, said, "Ah, you dear children, what has brought you here? Come in and stay with me, and no harm shall befall you!" and so saying, she took them both by the hand and led them into her cottage. A good meal of milk and pancakes, with sugar, apples, and nuts, was spread on the table, and in the back room were two nice little beds, covered with white, where Hansel and Gretel laid themselves down, and thought they were in heaven.

The old woman behaved very kindly to them, but in reality she was a wicked witch who waylaid children. She had built the bread house in order to entice them in, but as soon as they were in her power she killed them, cooked and ate them, and made a great festival of the day. Witches have red eyes and cannot see very far, but they have a fine sense of smell, like wild beasts, so that they know when children approach them. When Hansel and Gretel had come near the witch's house, she had laughed wickedly, saying, "Here come two who will not escape me." And early in the morning, before they awoke, she went up to them and saw how lovingly they lay sleeping, with their chubby red cheeks, and she mumbled to herself, "That will be a good bite." Then she seized Hansel with her rough hands and shut him up in a little cage with a lattice door, and although he screamed loudly it was of no use. Gretel came next, and, shaking her, the witch said, "Get up, you lazy thing, and fetch some water to cook something good for your brother. He must stay in that cage and get fat—when he is fat enough I shall eat him." Gretel began to cry, but it was all useless, for the old witch made her do as she wished. So a nice meal was cooked for Hansel, but Gretel got nothing but a crab's claw.

Every morning the old witch came to the cage and said, "Hansel, stretch out your finger so I may feel whether you are getting fat." But Hansel used to stretch out a bone, and the old woman, having very bad sight, thought it was his finger, and wondered very much that he did not get fatter. When four weeks had passed and Hansel still seemed quite lean, she lost all patience and would not

wait any longer. "Gretel," she called out in a passion, "get some water quickly. Whether Hansel is fat or lean, this morning I will kill him and cook him." Oh, how the poor little sister grieved as she was forced to fetch the water! The tears ran fast down her cheeks. "Dear good God, help us now!" she exclaimed. "If we had been eaten by the wild beasts in the wood, at least we would have died together." But the old witch called out, "Stop that noise! It won't help you a bit."

So early in the morning Gretel was forced to go out and fill the kettle and make a fire. "First we will bake, however," said the old woman. "I have already heated the oven and kneaded the dough," and so saying, she pushed poor Gretel up to the oven, where the flames were burning fiercely. "Creep in," said the witch, "and see if it is hot enough, and then we will put in the bread," but she intended, when Gretel got in, to shut up the oven and let her bake, so that she might eat her as well as Hansel. Gretel perceived what her thoughts were and said, "I do not know how to do it—how shall I get in?" "You stupid goose!" said the witch. "The opening is big enough. See, I could even get in myself!" and she got up and put her head into the oven. Then Gretel gave her a push, so that she fell right in, and then Gretel shut the iron door and bolted it. Oh, how horribly the wicked witch howled, but Gretel ran away and left her to burn to ashes.

Now she ran to Hansel, forced his door open, and called out, "Hansel, we are saved—the old witch is dead!" So he sprang out, like a bird out of his cage when the door is opened, and they were so glad that they fell on each other's neck and kissed each other over and over again. And now, as there was nothing to fear, they went into the witch's house, where in every corner were caskets full of pearls and precious stones. "These are better than pebbles," said Hansel, putting as many into his pocket as it would hold, while Gretel thought, "I will take some home too," and filled her apron full. "We must be off now," said Hansel, "and get out of this enchanted forest."

But when they had walked for two hours they came to a large expanse of water. "We cannot get across," said Hansel. "I can see no bridge at all." "And there is no boat either," said Gretel, "but there is a white duck swimming. I will ask her to help us over," and she sang:

> *"Little Duck, good little Duck,*
> *Gretel and Hansel, here we stand;*
> *There is neither stile nor bridge.*
> *Take us on your back to land."*

So the duck came to them, and Hansel sat himself on the duck's back and bade his sister sit behind him. "No," answered Gretel, "that will be too much for the duck. She will take us over one at a time." This the good duck did, and when both had happily reached the other side and had walked a little way, they came to a familiar wood, which they knew better with every step they took, and at last they saw their father's house. Then they began to run. They burst into the house and fell on their father's neck. He had not had one happy hour since he had left the children in the forest, and his wife was dead. Gretel shook her apron, and the pearls and precious stones rolled out on the floor, and Hansel threw down one handful after another out of his pocket. Then all their sorrows were ended, and they lived together in great happiness.

CHERRY, OR THE FROG BRIDE

N a far-off land there was once a King who had three sons. Not far from his kingdom lived an old woman who had an only daughter, called Cherry. The King sent his sons out to see the world, so they might learn the ways of foreign lands and get wisdom and skill in ruling the kingdom that they were one day to have for their own. But the old woman lived in peace at home with her daughter, who was called Cherry, because she liked cherries better than any other food, and would eat scarcely anything else. Now her poor old mother had no garden, and no money to buy cherries every day for her daughter, and at last there was no plan left but to go to a neighboring nunnery garden and beg the finest cherries she could get of the nuns, for she dared not let her daughter go out by herself, as she was very pretty and she feared some mischance might befall her. Cherry's taste was, however, very well known, and as it happened that the Abbess was as fond of cherries as she was, it was soon discovered where all the best fruit went, and the Holy Mother was not a little angry at missing some of her stock and finding where it had gone.

The Princes, while wandering on, came one day to the town where Cherry and her mother lived, and as they passed along the street they saw the fair maiden standing at the window, combing her long, beautiful locks of hair. Each of the three fell deeply in love with her, and each one said how much he longed to have her for his wife! Scarcely had the wish been spoken when all drew their swords, and a dreadful battle began. The fight lasted a long time, and their rage grew hotter and hotter until at last the Abbess, hearing the uproar, came to the gate. When she discovered that her neighbor was the cause, her old spite against her broke out, and in her rage she wished that Cherry was turned into an ugly frog sitting in the water under the bridge at the world's end. No sooner said than done—poor Cherry became a frog and vanished from their sight. The Princes now had nothing to fight about, so, sheathing their swords again, they shook hands as brothers and went on toward their father's home.

The old King meanwhile found that he was growing weak and ill-fitted for the business of reigning. He thought of giving up his kingdom, but to whom should he give it? This was a point that his fatherly heart could not settle, for he loved all his sons equally. "My dear children," said he, "I grow old and weak, and I would like to give up my kingdom, but I cannot make up my mind which of you to choose for my heir, for I love all three of you. Besides, I would want to give my people the cleverest and best of you for their King. However, I will give you three trials, and the one who wins the prize will have the kingdom. The first is to seek me out one hundred yards of cloth, so fine that I can draw it through my gold ring." The sons said they would do their best, and set out on the search.

The two eldest brothers took with them many followers, and coaches and horses of all sorts, to bring home all the beautiful cloths they might find, but the youngest went alone. They soon came to where the roads branched off in several directions; two ran through smiling meadows, with smooth paths and shady groves, but the third looked dreary and dirty and went over barren wastes. The two eldest chose the pleasant ways, and the youngest took his leave and whistled along over the dreary road. Whenever fine linen was to be seen, the two elder brothers bought it, and bought so much that their coaches and horses bent under their burden. The youngest, on the other hand, journeyed on many a weary day and found not a place where he could buy even one piece of cloth that was at all fine and good. His heart sank, and with every mile he grew more and more heavy and sorrowful. At last he came to a bridge over a stream, and there he sat himself down to rest and sigh over his bad luck. An ugly-looking frog popped its head out of the water and asked, in a voice that was not at all a harsh sound in his ears what was the matter. The Prince said impatiently, "Silly frog! You cannot help me." "Who told you so?" said the frog. "Tell me what's wrong." After a while the Prince opened up with the whole story and told why his father had sent him out. "I will help you," said the frog, and it jumped back into the stream and soon came back, dragging a small piece of linen not bigger than one's hand, and by no means the cleanest in the world. However, there it was, and the Prince was told to take it away with him. He had no great liking for such a dirty rag, but there was something in the frog's speech that pleased him very much, and he thought to himself, "It can do no harm, it is better than nothing." So he picked it up, put it in his pocket, and thanked the frog. The frog dived down again, panting and quite tired, it seemed, from its work. The farther the Prince went the heavier he found, to his great joy, the pocket grew, and so he turned himself homeward, trusting greatly in his good luck.

He reached home about the same time that his brothers came up, with their horses and coaches all heavily laden. The old King was very glad to see his children again, and he pulled the ring off his finger to see who had done the best, but in all the stock the two eldest sons had brought back there was not one piece a tenth part of which would go through the ring. At this they were greatly abashed, for they had laughed at their brother, who had come home, as they thought, empty-handed. But how great was their anger when they saw him pull from his pocket a piece that, for softness, beauty, and whiteness, was a thousand times better than anything ever before seen! It was so fine that it passed with ease through the ring; indeed, two such pieces would readily have gone through it together. The father embraced the lucky youth, told his servants to throw the coarse cloth into the sea, and said to his children, "Now you must set about the second task which I assign to you. Bring me home a little dog, so small that it will lie in a nutshell."

His sons were quite frightened at such a task, but they all longed for the crown, and made up their minds to try for it, and so after a few days they set out once more on their travels. At the crossroads they parted as before, and the youngest chose his old, dreary, rugged road with all the bright hopes that his former good luck gave him. He had scarcely sat down again at the foot of the bridge when his old friend the frog jumped out, set itself beside him, and as before opened its big, wide mouth and croaked out, "What is the matter?" This time the Prince had no doubt about the frog's power and therefore told what he wanted. "It shall be done for you," said the frog. It sprang into the stream and soon brought up a hazelnut, laid it at his feet, and told him to take it home to his father, crack it gently, and then see what happened. The Prince went his way very well pleased, and the frog, tired from its task, jumped back into the water.

His brothers had reached home first and had brought with them a great many very pretty little dogs. The old King, willing to help them all he could, sent for a large walnut shell and tried it with every one of the little dogs, but one stuck fast with the hind foot out, and another with the head, and a third with the forefoot, and a fourth with its tail—in short, some one way and some another, but none were at all likely to sit easily in this new kind of kennel. When all had been tried, the youngest son bowed dutifully before his father and gave him the hazelnut, begging him to crack it very carefully. The moment this was done, out ran a beautiful little white dog on the King's hand, wagged its tail, fondled his new master, and soon turned around and barked at the other little beasts in the most graceful manner, to the delight of the whole court. The joy of everyone was great; the old King again embraced his lucky son, told his people to drown all the other dogs in the sea, and said to his children, "Dear sons, your weightiest tasks are now over. Listen to my last wish: whoever brings home the fairest lady shall be at once the heir to my crown."

The prize was so tempting and the opportunity so fair for all that none had any doubts about setting out, each in his own way, to try to be the winner. The youngest was not in such good spirits as he had been the last time; he thought to himself, "The old frog has been able to do a great deal for me, but all its power can be of no use to me now, for where would it find me a fair maiden, much less a fairer maiden than was ever seen at my father's court? The swamps where it lives have no living things in them except toads, snakes, and such creatures." Meantime he went on, and sighed with a heavy heart as he sat down again by the bridge. "Ah, Frog!" said he. "This time you can do me no good." "Never mind," croaked the frog. "Just tell me what is the matter now." Then the Prince told his old friend what trouble had now come upon him. "Go home," said the frog. "The fair maiden will follow you, but take care that you do not laugh at whatever may happen!" The frog then sprang into the water and was soon out of sight.

The Prince sighed again, for he trusted the frog's word very little this time. But he had not gone many steps toward home before he heard a noise behind him and, looking around, saw six large water rats dragging along at full trot a large pumpkin shaped like a coach. On the box sat an old fat toad as coachman, and behind stood two little frogs as footmen, and two fine mice with stately whiskers ran before as outriders. Within sat his old friend the frog, rather misshapen and unseemly, to be sure, but still with a somewhat graceful air as it bowed to him in passing. Much too deeply concerned as to his chance of finding the fair lady he was seeking to take heed of the strange scene before him, the Prince scarcely looked at it and was even less inclined to laugh. The coach passed on a little way and soon turned a corner that hid it from his sight, but how astonished was he, on turning the corner himself, to find a handsome coach and six black horses standing there, with a coachman in smart livery, and within the coach was the most beautiful lady he had ever seen, whom he soon knew to be the fair Cherry, for whom his heart had so longed. As he came up, the servants opened the coach door, and he was allowed to seat himself beside the beautiful lady.

They soon came to his father's city, where his brothers also arrived with trains of fair ladies, but as soon as Cherry was seen, the court gave her, without question, the crown of beauty. The delighted father embraced his son and named him heir to his throne and ordered all the other ladies to be thrown, like the little dogs, into the sea and drowned. Then the Prince married Cherry and lived long and happily with her, and indeed lives with her still—if he is not dead.

THE FISHERMAN AND HIS WIFE

N a hovel close by the sea a poor fisher-man lived with his wife. He spent all day long fishing, and one morning, as he sat on the shore with his rod, looking at the shining water and watching his line, all of a sudden his float was dragged away deep under the sea, and in drawing it up he pulled a great fish out of the water. The fish said to him, "Pray let me live. I am not a real fish—I am an enchanted Prince. Put me in the water again and let me go." "Oh," said the man, "you don't have to use so many words to explain it all. I don't want to have anything to do

with a fish that can talk, so swim away as soon as you please." Then he put him back into the water, and the fish darted straight down to the bottom, leaving a long streak of blood behind him.

When the fisherman went home to his wife in their hovel, he told her how he had caught a great fish and how it had told him it was an enchanted Prince, and that on hearing it speak he had let it go again. "Didn't you ask it for anything?" said the wife. "No," said the man. "What should I ask for?" "Ah!" said the wife. "We live wretchedly here in this nasty, stinking hut! Go back and tell the fish we want a little cottage."

The fisherman did not like the idea very much. However, he went to the sea, and when he got there the water looked all yellow and green. And he stood at the water's edge and said:

"O man of the sea!
Come listen to me,
For Alice, my wife,
The plague of my life,
Hath sent me to beg a boon of thee!"

Then the fish came swimming to him and said, "Well, what does she want?" "Ah!" answered the fisherman. "My wife says that when I caught you, I should have asked you for something before I let you go again. She does not want to live any longer in the hut— she wants a little cottage." "Go home, then," said the fish. "She is in the cottage already." So the man went home and saw his wife standing at the door of a cottage. "Come in, come in," said she. "Isn't this much better than the hut?" And there was a parlor and a bedroom and a kitchen, and behind the cottage there was a little garden with all sorts of flowers and fruit, and a courtyard full of ducks and chickens. "Ah!" said the fisherman. "How happy we'll be here!" "We will try to be, at least," said his wife.

Everything went right for a week or two, and then Dame Alice said, "Husband, there is not room enough in this cottage—the courtyard and garden are much too small. I would like to have a large stone castle to live in, so go to the fish again and tell him to give us a castle." "Wife," said the fisherman, "I don't like to go to him again. He may be angry. We should be content with the cottage." "Nonsense!" said the wife. "He will do it very willingly. Go on and try."

The fisherman went, but his heart was heavy, and when he came to the sea, it looked blue and gloomy, though it was quite calm. And he went close to it, and said:

"O man of the sea!
Come listen to me,
For Alice, my wife,
The plague of my life,
Hath sent me to beg a boon of thee!"

"Well, what does she want now?" said the fish. "Ah!" said the man very sorrowfully. "My wife wants to live in a stone castle." "Go home, then," said the fish. "She is standing at the door of it already." So away went the fisherman and found his wife standing before a great castle. "See," said she, "is this not grand?" With that they went into the castle together and found a great many servants there, and the rooms all richly furnished and full of golden chairs and tables, and behind the castle was a garden, and a wood half a mile long, full of sheep and goats and hares and deer, and in the courtyard were stables and cow barns. "Well," said the man, "now we will live contented and happy in this beautiful castle for the rest of our lives." "Perhaps," said the wife, "but let us consider and sleep on it before we make up our minds." So they went to bed.

The next morning when Dame Alice awoke, it was broad daylight, and she jogged the fisherman with her elbow and said, "Get up, Husband, and bestir yourself, for we must be King of all the land." "Wife, Wife," said the man, "why should we wish to be King? I will not be King." "Then I will," said Alice. "But, Wife," answered the fisherman, "how can you be King? The fish cannot make you a King." "Husband," said she, "say no more about it, but go and try—I will be King!" So the man went away, quite sorrowful to think that his wife should want to be King. The sea looked a dark gray and was covered with foam as he cried out:

> *"O man of the sea!*
> *Come listen to me,*
> *For Alice, my wife,*
> *The plague of my life,*
> *Hath sent me to beg a boon of thee!"*

"Well, what would she have now?" said the fish. "Alas!" said the man. "My wife wants to be King." "Go home," said the fish. "She is King already."

Then the fisherman went home, and as he came close to the palace, he saw a troop of soldiers and heard the sound of drums and trumpets, and when he entered, he saw his wife sitting on a high throne of gold and diamonds, with a golden crown on her head, and on each side of her stood six beautiful maidens, each a head taller than the other. "Well, Wife," said the fisherman, "are you King?" "Yes," said she, "I am King." And when he had looked at her for a long time, he said, "Ah, Wife, what a fine thing it is to be King! Now we shall never have anything more to wish for." "I don't know how that may be," said she. "Never is a long time. I am King, it's true, but I'm beginning to be tired of it, and I think I would like to be Emperor." "Alas, Wife, why would you want to be Emperor?" said the fisherman. "Husband," said she, "go to the fish. I say I will be Emperor." "Ah, Wife," replied the fisherman, "the fish cannot make you an Emperor, and I would not like to ask for such a thing." "I am King," said Alice, "and you are my slave, so go at once!" So the fisherman was obliged to go, and he muttered as he went along, "This will come to no good. It is too much to ask. The fish will be tired at last, and then we will be sorry for what we have done."

He soon arrived at the sea, and the water was quite black and muddy, and a mighty whirlwind blew over it, but he went to the shore and said:

> *"O man of the sea!*
> *Come listen to me,*
> *For Alice, my wife,*
> *The plague of my life,*
> *Hath sent me to beg a boon of thee!"*

"What would she have now!" said the fish. "Ah!" said the fisherman. "She wants to be Emperor." "Go home," said the fish. "She is Emperor already."

So he went home again, and as he came near he saw his wife sitting on a very lofty throne made of solid gold, with a great crown on her head fully two yards high, and on each side of her stood her guards and attendants in a row, each one smaller than the other, from the tallest giant down to a little dwarf no bigger than my finger. And before her stood princes and dukes and earls, and the fisherman went up to her and said, "Wife, are you Emperor?" "Yes," said she, "I am Emperor." "Ah!" said the man as he gazed upon her. "What a fine thing it is to be Emperor!" "Husband," said she, "why should we stay at being Emperor? I will be Pope next." "Oh, Wife, Wife!" said he. "How can you be Pope? There is only one Pope at a time in Christendom." "Husband," said she, "I will be Pope this very day." "But," replied the husband, "the fish cannot make you Pope." "What nonsense!" said she. "If he can make an emperor, he can make a Pope—go and try him."

So the fisherman went. But when he came to the shore, the wind was raging, and the sea was tossed up and down like boiling water, and the ships were in the greatest distress and danced upon the waves most fearfully. In the middle of the sky there was a little blue, but toward the south it was all red, as if a dreadful storm were rising. At this the fisherman was terribly frightened and trembled, so that his knees knocked together, but he went to the shore and said:

41

"O man of the sea!
Come listen to me,
For Alice, my wife,
The plague of my life,
Hath sent me to beg a boon of thee!"

"What does she want now?" said the fish. "Ah!" said the fisherman. "My wife wants to be Pope." "Go home," said the fish. "She is Pope already."

Then the fisherman went home and found his wife sitting on a throne that was two miles high, and she had three great crowns on her head, and around stood all the pomp and power of the Church, and on each side were two rows of burning lights, of all sizes, the greatest as large as the highest and biggest tower in the world, and the least no larger than a small rushlight. "Wife," said the fisherman as he looked at all this grandeur, "are you Pope?" "Yes," said she, "I am Pope." "Well, Wife," replied he, "it is a grand thing to be Pope, and now you must be content, for you can be nothing greater." "I will consider that," said the wife. Then they went to bed, but Dame Alice could not sleep all night for thinking what she should be next. At last morning came, and the sun rose. "Ha!" thought she as she looked at it through the window. "Cannot I prevent the sun from rising?" At this she was very angry, and she wakened her husband and said, "Husband, go to the fish and tell him I want to be lord of the sun and the moon." The fisherman was half asleep, but the thought frightened him so much that he started and fell out of bed. "Alas, Wife!" said he. "Can't you be content to be Pope?" "No," said she, "I am very uneasy, and cannot bear to see the sun and moon rise without my leave. Go to the fish right away."

Then the man went, trembling with fear, and as he was going down to the shore a dreadful storm arose, so that the trees and the rocks shook, and the heavens became black, and the lightning played, and the thunder rolled, and you might have seen in the sea great black waves like mountains with a white crown of foam upon them, and the fisherman said:

"O man of the sea!
Come listen to me,
For Alice, my wife,
The plague of my life,
Hath sent me to beg a boon of thee!"

"What does she want now?" said the fish. "Ah!" said he. "She wants to be lord of the sun and moon." "Go home," said the fish, "to your hut again!" And there they live to this very day.

ROSEBUD

 T happened, once upon a time, that a King and Queen had no children, and this they lamented very much. But one day as the Queen was walking by the side of the river, a little fish lifted its head out of the water and said, "Your wish shall be fulfilled, and you shall soon have a daughter." What the little fish had foretold soon came to pass, and the Queen had a little girl who was so very beautiful that the King could not cease looking at her for joy, and he determined to hold a great feast. So he invited not only his relations, friends, and neighbors, but also all the fairies, that they might be kind and good to his little daughter.

Now there were thirteen fairies in his kingdom, and he had only twelve golden dishes for them to eat out of, so that he was obliged to leave one of the fairies without an invitation. The rest came, and after the feast was over they gave all their best gifts to the little Princess. One gave her virtue, another beauty, another riches, and so on till she had all that was excellent in the world. When eleven had finished blessing her, the thirteenth, who had not been invited and was very angry on that account, came in, and determined to have her revenge. So she cried out, "The King's daughter shall in her fifteenth year be wounded by a spindle and fall down dead." Then the twelfth, who had not yet given her gift, came forward and said that the bad wish must be fulfilled, but that she could soften it, and that the King's daughter should not die, but fall asleep for a hundred years.

But the King hoped to save his dear child from the threatened evil, and ordered that all the spindles in the kingdom should be bought up and destroyed. All the fairies' gifts were in the meantime fulfilled, for the Princess was so beautiful and well-behaved and amiable and wise that everyone who knew her loved her. Now it happened that on the very day she was fifteen years old the King and Queen were not at home, and she was left alone in the palace. So she roved about by herself and looked at all the rooms and chambers till at last she came to an old tower, to which there was a narrow staircase ending with a little door. In the door there was a golden key, and when she turned it the door sprang open, and there sat an old lady spinning away very busily. "Why, how now, good mother," said the Princess, "what are you doing there?" "Spinning," said the old lady, and nodded her head. "How prettily that little thing turns around!" said the Princess, and took the spindle and began to spin. But scarcely had she touched it before the prophecy was fulfilled, and she fell down lifeless on the floor.

However, she was not dead, but had only fallen into a deep sleep, and the King and the Queen, who just then came home, and all their court, fell asleep too, and the horses slept in the stables, and the dogs in the courtyard, the pigeons on the housetop and the flies on the walls. Even the fire on the hearth left off blazing and went to sleep, and the meat that was roasting stood still, and the cook, who was at that moment pulling the kitchen boy by the hair to box his ears for something he had done wrong, let him go, and both fell asleep, and so everything stood still and slept soundly.

A large hedge of thorns soon grew around the palace, and every year it became higher and thicker, till at last the whole palace was surrounded and hidden, and not even the roof or the chimneys could be seen. But there went a report through all the land of the beautiful sleeping Rosebud (for so was the King's daughter called), so that from time to time several Kings' sons came and tried to break through the thicket into the palace. This they could never do, for the thorns and bushes laid hold of them as if with hands, and there they stuck fast and died miserably.

After many, many years there came a King's son into that land, and an old man told him the story of the thicket of thorns, and how a beautiful palace stood behind it, in which was a wondrous Princess called Rosebud, asleep with all her court. He told, too, how he had heard from his grandfather that many, many Princes had come and had tried to break through the thicket, but had stuck fast and died. Then the young Prince said, "All this shall not frighten me. I will go and see Rosebud." The old man tried to dissuade him, but he persisted in going.

Now that very day the hundred years were completed, and as the Prince came to the thicket, he saw nothing but beautiful flowering shrubs, through which he passed with ease, and they closed after him as firm as ever. Then he came at last to the palace, and there in the courtyard lay the dogs asleep, and the horses in the stables, and on the roof sat the pigeons fast asleep with their heads under their wings, and when he came into the palace, the flies slept on the walls, and the cook in the kitchen was still holding up her hand as if she would beat the boy, and the maid sat with a black fowl in her hand ready to be plucked.

Then he went on still farther, and all was so still that he could hear every breath he drew, till at last he came to the old tower and opened the door of the little room in which Rosebud was, and there she lay fast asleep, and looked so beautiful that he could not take his eyes off her, and he stooped down and gave her a kiss. But the moment he kissed her she opened her eyes and awoke and smiled at him. Then they went out together, and presently the King and Queen also awoke, and all the court, and they gazed at each other with great wonder. And the horses got up and shook themselves, and the dogs jumped about and barked; the pigeons took their heads from under their wings and looked about and flew into the fields; the flies on the walls buzzed away; the fire in the kitchen blazed up and cooked the dinner, and the roast meat turned around again; the cook gave the boy a box on his ear so that he cried out, and the maid went on plucking the fowl. And then was the wedding of the Prince and Rosebud celebrated, and they lived happily together all their lives long.

THE GOOSE GIRL

NTOLD ages ago a King died much before his time, leaving a gentle Queen and a beautiful daughter. When the child grew up, she was betrothed to a Prince who lived a great way off, and as the time drew near for her to be married, she got ready to set off on her journey to his country. Then the Queen, her mother, packed up a great many costly things: jewels, and gold, and silver; trinkets, fine dresses—in short, everything that became a royal bride—for she loved her child very dearly, and she gave her a waiting maid to ride with her and deliver her into the bridegroom's hands, and each had a horse for the journey. Now the Princess's horse was called Falada and could speak.

When the time came for them to set out, the old Queen went into her bedchamber and took a little knife and cut off a lock of her hair and gave it to her daughter and said, "Take care of it, dear child, for it is a charm that may be of use to you on the road." Then they took a sorrowful leave of each other, and the Princess put the lock of her mother's hair in her bosom, got on her horse, and set off on her journey to her bridegroom's kingdom.

One day, as they were riding along by the side of a brook, the Princess began to feel very thirsty and said to her maid, "Pray get down and fetch me some water in my golden cup out of yonder brook, for I want to drink." "Nay," said the maid, "if you are thirsty, get down yourself and lie down by the water and drink. I shall not be your waiting maid any longer." The Princess was so thirsty that she got down and knelt over the little brook and drank, for she was frightened and dared not bring out her golden cup, and then she wept and said, "Alas! What will become of me?" And the lock of hair answered her, and said:

> *"Alas! Alas! If thy mother knew it,*
> *Sadly, sadly her heart would rue it."*

But the Princess was very humble and meek, so she said nothing of her maid's bad behavior, but got on her horse again.

They rode farther on their journey till the day grew so warm and the sun so scorching that the bride began to feel very thirsty again, and at last when they came to a river she forgot her maid's rude speech and said, "Pray get down and fetch me some water to drink in my golden cup." But the maid answered her and spoke even more haughtily than before. "Drink if you will, but I will not be your waiting maid." Then the Princess was so thirsty that she got off her horse and lay down and held her head over the running stream and cried and said, "What will become of me?" And the lock of hair answered her again:

> *"Alas! Alas! If thy mother knew it,*

Sadly, sadly her heart would rue it."

And as she leaned down to drink, the lock of hair fell from her bosom and floated away with the water without her seeing it, she was so frightened. But her maid saw it and was very glad, for she knew the charm and saw that the poor bride would be in her power now that she had lost the lock of hair. So when the bride had finished drinking and would have gotten on Falada again, the maid said, "I shall ride upon Falada, and you may have my horse instead," so she was forced to give up her horse and soon afterward to take off her royal clothes and put on her maid's shabby ones.

At last, as they drew near the end of their journey, this treacherous servant threatened to kill her mistress if she ever told anyone what had happened. But Falada saw it all and marked it well. Then the waiting maid got on Falada, and the real bride was set upon the other horse, and they went on in this way till at last they came to the royal court. There was great joy at their coming, and the Prince flew to meet them and lifted the maid from her horse, thinking she was the one who was to be his wife, and she was led upstairs to the royal chamber, but the true Princess was told to stay in the courtyard below.

But the old King happened to be looking out of the window and saw her in the yard below, and as she looked very pretty and too delicate for a waiting maid, he went into the royal chamber to ask the bride who it was she had brought with her and was thus left standing in the courtyard below. "I brought her with me for the sake of her company on the road," said she. "Pray give the girl some work to do so she may not be idle." For some time the old King could not think of any work for her to do, but at last he said, "I have a lad who takes care of my geese—she may go and help him." Now the name of this lad the real bride was to help in watching the King's geese was Curdken.

Soon after, the false bride said to the Prince, "Dear Husband, pray do me one piece of kindness." "That I will," said the Prince.

"Then tell one of your slaughterers to cut off the head of the horse I rode on, for it was very unruly and plagued me sadly on the road," but the truth was, she was very much afraid lest Falada should speak and tell everything she had done to the Princess. She carried her point, and the faithful Falada was killed, but when the true Princess heard of it, she wept and begged the man to nail Falada's head against a large dark gate of the city, through which she had to pass every morning and evening, so that there she might still see him sometimes. Then the slaughterer said he would do as she wished, and he cut off the head and nailed it fast under the dark gate.

Early the next morning, as she and Curdken went out through the gate, she said sorrowfully:

"Falada, Falada, there thou art hanging!"

and the head answered:

"Bride, bride, there thou art ganging!
Alas! Alas! If thy mother knew it,
Sadly, sadly her heart would rue it."

Then they went out of the city and drove the geese on. And when she came to the meadow, she sat down on a bank there and let down her waving locks of hair, which were all of pure silver, and when Curdken saw it glitter in the sun, he ran up and would have pulled some of the locks out, but she cried:

"Blow, breezes, blow!
Let Curdken's hat go!
Blow, breezes, blow!
Let him after it go!
O'er hills, dales, and rocks,
Away be it whirled,
Till the silvery locks
Are all combed and curled!"

Then there came a wind so strong that it blew off Curdken's hat, and away it flew over the hills, and he after it, till, by the time he came back, she had finished combing and curling her hair and

54

put it up again safe. Then Curdken was very angry and sulky and would not speak to her at all, but they watched the geese until it grew dark in the evening, and then drove them homeward.

The next morning, as they were going through the dark gate, the poor girl looked up at Falada's head, and cried:

"Falada, Falada, there thou art hanging!"

and it answered:

"Bride, bride, there thou art ganging!
Alas! Alas! If thy mother knew it,
Sadly, sadly her heart would rue it."

Then she drove the geese on and sat down again in the meadow and began to comb out her hair as before. Curdken ran up to her and wanted to take hold of it, but she cried out quickly:

"Blow, breezes, blow!
Let Curdken's hat go!
Blow, breezes, blow!
Let him after it go!
O'er hills, dales, and rocks,
Away be it whirled,
Till the silvery locks
Are all combed and curled!"

Then the wind came and blew his hat, and off it flew a great way, over the hills and far away, so that he had to run after it, and when he came back, she had done up her hair again, and all was safe. So they watched the geese till it grew dark.

In the evening, after they came home, Curdken went to the old King and said, "I cannot have that strange girl to help me to keep the geese any longer." "Why?" said the King. "Because she does nothing but tease me all day long." Then the King made him tell everything that had happened. And Curdken said, "When we go in the morning through the dark gate with our flock of geese, she weeps and talks with the head of a horse that hangs upon the wall, and says:

'Falada, Falada, there thou art hanging!'

and the head answers:

'Bride, bride, there thou art ganging!
Alas! Alas! If thy mother knew it,
Sadly, sadly her heart would rue it.'"

And Curdken went on telling the King what had happened in the meadow where the geese fed, and how his hat was blown away and he was forced to run after it and leave his flock. But the old King told him to go out again as usual the next day, and when morning came, the King placed himself behind the dark gate and heard how she spoke to Falada and how Falada answered, and then he went into the field and hid himself in a bush by the meadow's side and soon saw with his own eyes how they drove the flock of geese and how, after a little time, she let down her hair that glittered in the sun, and then he heard her say:

"Blow, breezes, blow!
Let Curdken's hat go!
Blow, breezes, blow!
Let him after it go!
O'er hills, dales, and rocks,
Away be it whirled,
Till the silvery locks
Are all combed and curled!"

And soon came a gale of wind and carried away Curdken's hat while the girl went on combing and curling her hair. All this the old King saw, and he went home without being seen, and when the little goose girl came back in the evening, he called her aside and asked her why she did so, but she burst into tears and said, "That I must not tell you or any man, or I shall lose my life."

But the old King begged so hard that she had no peace till she had told him all, word for word, and it was very lucky for her that she did so, for the King ordered royal clothes to be put upon her and gazed on her with wonder, she was so beautiful. Then he called his son and told him that he had only the false bride, for she was merely a waiting maid, while the true one stood by. And the young Prince rejoiced when he saw her beauty and heard how meek and patient she had been, and, without saying anything, he ordered a great feast to be made ready for all his court. The bridegroom sat at the top, with the false Princess on one side and the true one on the other, but nobody knew her, for she was quite dazzling to their eyes and was not at all like the little goose girl, now that she had her brilliant dress.

When they had eaten and drunk and were very merry, the old King told the story, as one that he had once heard of, and asked the true waiting maid what she thought should be done to anyone who would behave thus. "Nothing better," said this false bride, "than that she should be thrown into a cask stuck with sharp nails, and that two white horses should be put to it and should drag it from street to street till she is dead." "You are she!" said the old King. "And since you have judged yourself, it shall be so done to you." And the Prince was married to his true wife, and they reigned over the kingdom in peace and happiness all their lives.

CATSKIN

NCE upon a time there was a King whose Queen had hair of the purest gold and who was so beautiful that her match was not to be met with on the whole face of the earth. But this beautiful Queen fell ill, and when she felt that her end drew near, she called the King to her and said, "Vow to me that you will never marry again unless you find a wife who is as beautiful as I am and who has golden hair like mine." Then when the King in his grief had vowed all she asked, she closed her eyes and died. But the King was not to be comforted and for a long time never thought of taking another wife. At last, however, his counselors said, "This

will not do; the King must marry again so we may have a Queen."
So messengers were sent far and wide to seek a bride who was as
beautiful as the late Queen. But there was no Princess in the world
so beautiful, and if there had been, still there was not one to be
found who had such golden hair. So the messengers came home,
having done all their work for nothing.

Now the King had a daughter who was just as beautiful as her
mother and had the same golden hair. And when she was grown
up, the King looked at her and saw that she was just like his late
Queen. Then he said to his courtiers, "May I not marry my daughter? She is the very image of my dead wife. Unless I have her, I shall
not find any bride upon the whole earth, and you say there must be
a Queen." When the courtiers heard this, they were shocked and
said, "Heaven forbid that a father should marry his daughter! Out
of so great a sin no good can come." And his daughter was also
shocked but hoped the King would soon give up such thoughts, so
she said to him, "Before I marry anyone I must have three dresses.
One must be of gold like the sun, another must be of shining silver
like the moon, and a third must be dazzling as the stars. Besides
this, I want a mantle of a thousand different kinds of fur put together, to which every beast in the kingdom must give a part of his
skin." And thus she thought he would think of the matter no more.
But the King made the most skillful workmen in his kingdom weave
the three dresses, one as golden as the sun, another as silvery as the
moon, and a third shining like the stars, and his hunters were told
to hunt out all the beasts in his kingdom and take the finest furs out
of their skins, and so a mantle of a thousand furs was made.

When all was ready, the King sent them to her, but she got up
in the night when everyone was asleep, and she took three of her
trinkets—a golden ring, a golden necklace, and a golden brooch—
and packed the three dresses of the sun, moon, and stars up in a nutshell, and wrapped herself up in the mantle of all sorts of fur, and
smeared her face and hands with soot. Then she threw herself upon

Heaven for help in her need, and went away and journeyed the whole night, till at last she came to a large wood. As she was very tired, she sat down in the hollow of a tree and soon fell asleep, and there she slept till it was midday. And it happened that as the King to whom the wood belonged was hunting in it, his dogs came to the tree and began to snuff about and run around and around and then to bark. "Look sharp," said the King to the huntsmen, "and see what sort of game lies there." And the huntsmen went up to the tree, and when they came back again they said, "In the hollow tree there lies a most wonderful beast, such as we never saw before. Its skin seems of a thousand kinds of fur, but there it lies fast asleep." "See if you can catch it alive," said the King, "and we will take it with us." So the huntsmen took it up, and the maiden awoke and was greatly frightened, and said, "I am a poor child who has neither father nor mother left. Have pity on me and take me with you." Then they said, "Yes, Miss Catskin, you will do for the kitchen, you can sweep up the ashes and do things of that sort."

So they put her in the coach and took her home to the King's palace. Then they showed her a little room under the staircase where no light of day ever peeped in, and said, "Catskin, you may sleep there." And she was sent into the kitchen and made to fetch wood and water, to blow the fire, pluck the poultry, pick the herbs, sift the ashes, and do all the dirty work.

Thus Catskin lived for a long time very sorrowfully. "Ah, pretty Princess!" thought she, "What will now become of you?" But it happened one day that a feast was to be held in the King's castle, so she said to the cook, "May I go up a little while and see what is going on? I will take care to stand behind the door." And the cook said, "Yes, you may go, but be back again in half an hour's time to rake out the ashes." Then Catskin took her little lamp and went to her room and took off the fur skin, and washed the soot off her face and hands, so that her beauty shone forth like the sun from behind the clouds. She next opened her nutshell and brought out of it the dress that shone like the sun, and so went to the feast. Everyone made way for her, for nobody knew her, and they thought she could be no less than a King's daughter. But the King came up to her and held out his hand and danced with her, and he thought in his heart, "I never saw anyone half so beautiful."

When the dance came to an end, she curtsied, and when the King looked around for her she was gone, no one knew where. The guards who stood at the castle gate were called in, but they had seen no one. The truth was that she had run into her little room, pulled off her dress, blackened her face and hands, put on the fur-skin cloak, and was Catskin again. When she went into the kitchen to her work and began to rake the ashes, the cook said, "Let that alone till the morning, and make the King's soup. I would like to run up now and peek at the party, but take care you don't let a hair fall into it, or you will run the chance of never eating again."

As soon as the cook went away, Catskin made the King's soup and toasted a slice of bread as nicely as she could, and when it was ready, she went and looked in the room for her little golden ring and put it in the dish in which the soup was. When the dance was over, the King ordered his soup to be brought in, and it pleased him so well that he thought he had never tasted any so good before. At the bottom he saw a gold ring, and as he could not make out how it had gotten there, he ordered the cook to be sent for. The cook was frightened when she heard the summons, and said to Catskin, "You must have let a hair fall into the soup. If it is so, you will get a good beating." Then she went before the King, and he asked her who had made the soup. "I did," answered she. But the King said, "That is not true—it was better done than you could do it." Then she answered, "To tell the truth, I did not cook it, but Catskin did." "Then let Catskin come up," said the King, and when she came, he said to her, "Who are you?" "I am a poor child," said she, "who has lost both father and mother." "How did you happen to come to my palace?" he asked. "I am good for nothing," said she, "but to be a scullery girl and to have boots and shoes thrown at my head." "But how did you get the ring that was in the soup?" asked the King. But she would not admit that she knew anything about the ring, so the King sent her away again to go about her business.

After a time there was another feast, and Catskin asked the cook to let her go up and see it as before. "Yes," said she, "but come back again in half an hour and make for the King the soup that he likes so much." Then Catskin ran to her little room, washed herself quickly. and took out the dress that was silvery as the moon. She put it on, and when she went in looking like a King's daughter, the King went up to her and rejoiced at seeing her again, and when the dance began he danced with her. After the dance she managed to slip out so slyly that the King did not see where she had gone, but she ran into her little room and made herself into Catskin again, and went into the kitchen to make the soup. While the cook was upstairs, she got the golden necklace and dropped it into the soup. Then the soup was brought to the King, who ate it, and it pleased him as much as before, so he sent for the cook, who was again forced to tell him that Catskin had made it. Catskin was again brought before the King, but she still told him that she was fit only to have the boots and shoes thrown at her head.

When the King had ordered a feast to be gotten ready for the third time, it happened just the same as before. "You must be a witch, Catskin," said the cook, "for you always put something into the soup so that it pleases the King better than mine." However, she let Catskin go up as before. Then Catskin put on the dress that sparkled like the stars, and she went into the ballroom in it, and the King danced with her again and thought she had never looked so beautiful as she did then, so while he was dancing with her, he put a gold ring on her finger without her seeing it, and ordered that the dance should be kept up a long time. When it was at an end, he tried to hold her fast by the hand, but she slipped away and ran so quickly through the crowd that he lost sight of her, and she hurried as fast as she could into her little room under the stairs. But this time she had been away too long and had stayed beyond the half hour, so she had no time to take off her fine dress, but threw her fur mantle over it, and in her haste did not soot herself all over, but left one finger white.

Then she ran into the kitchen and made the King's soup, and as soon as the cook was gone, she put the golden brooch into the dish. When the King got to the bottom of the soup, he ordered Catskin to be called once more, and soon saw the white finger and the ring that he had put on it while they were dancing. He seized her hand and held it tightly, and when she tried to free herself and run away, the fur cloak fell off a little on one side, and the starry dress sparkled underneath it. Then he got hold of the fur and tore it off, and her golden hair and beautiful form were seen, and she could no longer hide herself, so she washed the soot and ashes from her face and showed herself to be the most beautiful Princess on the face of the earth. But the King said, "You are my beloved bride, and we will never more be parted from each other." And the wedding feast was held, and a merry day it was.

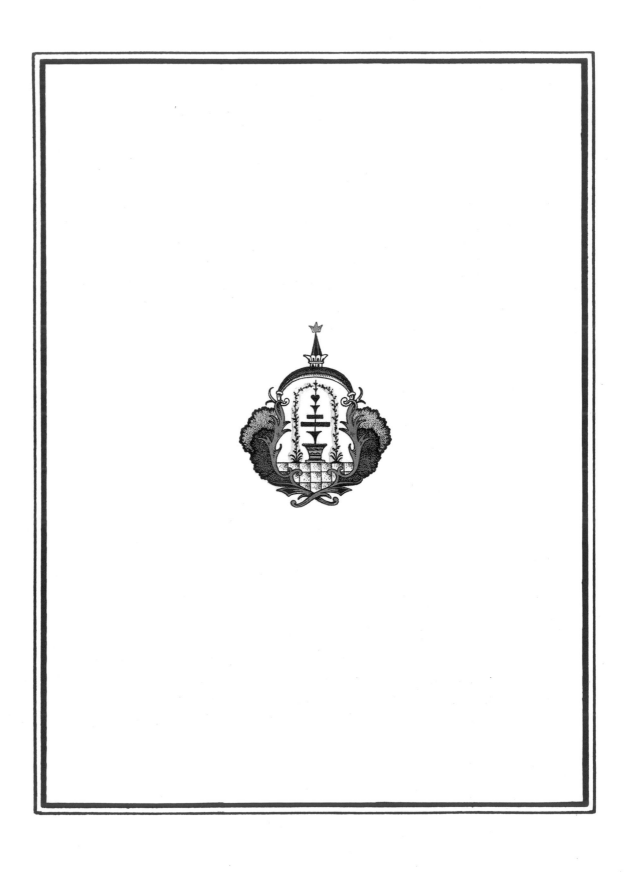

RUMPELSTILTSKIN

REAMING of wealth, a poor miller decided to better his lot. He had a very beautiful daughter who was also exceedingly shrewd and clever, and the miller was quite vain and proud of her. One day he told the King that his daughter could spin gold out of straw. Now this King was very fond of money, and when he heard the miller's boast, he was filled with avarice, and he ordered the girl to be brought before him. Then he led her to a chamber where there was a great quantity of straw, gave her a spinning wheel, and said, "All this must be spun into gold before morning, as you value your life." It was in vain that the poor maiden declared that she could do no such thing—the chamber was locked and she remained alone.

She sat down in one corner of the room and had begun to lament her hard fate when all of a sudden the door opened and a droll-looking little man hobbled in and said, "Good morrow to you, my good lass, what are you weeping for?" "Alas!" answered she. "I must spin this straw into gold, and I do not know how." "What will you give me," said the little man, "to do it for you?" "My necklace," replied the maiden. He took her at her word and sat himself down to the wheel; round about it went merrily, and presently the work was done and the gold all spun.

When the King came and saw this, he was greatly astonished and pleased, but his heart grew still greedier, and he shut up the poor miller's daughter again with another task. Then she did not know what to do, and sat down once more to weep, but the little man presently opened the door and said, "What will you give me to do your task?" "The ring on my finger," she replied. So her little friend took the ring and began to work at the wheel, till by the morning all was finished again.

The King was vastly delighted to see all this glittering treasure, but still he was not satisfied, and took the miller's daughter into a larger room and said, "All this must be spun tonight, and if you succeed, you shall be my Queen." As soon as she was alone the dwarf came in and said, "What will you give me to spin gold for you this third time?" "I have nothing left," said she. "Then promise me," said the little man, "your first child when you are Queen." "That may never be," thought the miller's daughter, and as she knew no other way to get her task done, she promised him what he asked, and he spun once more the whole heap of gold. The King came in the morning, and finding all he wanted, married her, and so the miller's daughter really became Queen.

At the birth of her first child the Queen rejoiced and forgot the little man and her promise, but one day he came into her chamber and reminded her of it. Then she grieved sorely at her misfortune and offered him all the treasures of the kingdom in exchange, but he would not agree. However, at last her tears softened

him, and he said, "I will give you three days' grace, and if during that time you tell me my name, you may keep your child."

Now the Queen lay awake all night, thinking of all the odd names that she had ever heard, and dispatched messengers all over the land to inquire after new ones. The next day the little man came, and she began with Timothy, Benjamin, Jeremiah, and all the other names she could remember, but to all of them he said, "That's not my name."

The second day she began with all the comical names she could hear of—Bandy-legs, Hunchback, Crook-shanks, and so on, but the little gentlemen still said to every one of them, "That's not my name."

The third day one of the messengers came back and said, "I have heard of no other name, but yesterday as I was climbing a high hill among the trees of the forest where the fox and the hare bid each other good night, I saw a little hut, and before the hut burned a fire, and around the fire danced a funny little man on one leg and sang:

"*Merrily the feast I'll make.*
Today I'll brew, tomorrow bake.
Merrily I'll dance and sing,
For next day will a stranger bring:
Little does my lady dream
Rumpelstiltskin is my name!"

When the Queen heard this, she jumped for joy, and as soon as her little visitor came and said, "Now, lady, what is my name?" "Is it John?" she asked. "No!" "Is it Tom?" "No!"

"Can your name be Rumpelstiltskin?"

"Some witch told you that! Some witch told you that!" cried the little man, and dashed his right foot in a rage so deep into the floor that he was forced to lay hold of his leg with both hands to pull it out. Then he made the best of things and went off, while everybody laughed at him for having had all his trouble for nothing.

THE VALIANT LITTLE TAILOR

"PRESERVES, good preserves for sale!" cried an old peasant woman as she came peddling her wares up the street one summer morning. Her cries fell on the ears of the village tailor, who was happily sewing away at the open window in his house. "Here, my good woman," the tailor called as he stuck his diminutive head out the window, "bring your wares right here!"

The woman mounted the three steps up to the tailor's house with her heavy basket and began to unpack all the pots before him. He looked at them all, held them up to the light, put his nose to them, and at last said, "These preserves appear to me to be very nice, so you may weigh me out four half-ounces, my good woman.

I don't mind even if you make it a quarter of a pound." The woman, who expected to have met with a good customer, gave him what he wished, and went away grumbling, very much dissatisfied.

"Now," exclaimed the tailor, "Heaven will send me a blessing on this preserve and give me fresh strength and vigor," and, taking the bread out of the cupboard, he cut himself a slice the size of the whole loaf and spread the preserve on it. "That will not taste at all bad," he said, "but before I have a bite, I will just get this waistcoat finished." So he laid the bread down near him and stitched away, making larger and larger stitches every time in his enthusiasm. Meanwhile the smell of the preserve mounted to the ceiling, where flies were sitting in great numbers, and enticed them down, so that soon a regular swarm of them had settled on the bread. "Hey, who invited you?" exclaimed the tailor, shooing away the unbidden guests, but the flies, not understanding his language, would not be driven off, and came again in greater numbers than before. This enraged the little man, and he snatched up a bag of cloth and brought it down upon them with an unmerciful swoop. When he raised it again, he counted no less than seven flies lying dead before him. "What a fellow you are!" said he to himself, wondering at his own bravery. "The whole town shall know of this." In great haste he cut himself out a band, hemmed it, and then put on it in large characters, "SEVEN AT ONE BLOW!" "Ah," said he, "not one city alone—the whole world shall know it!" and his heart fluttered with joy, like a lambkin's tail.

The little tailor bound the belt around his waist and prepared to travel forth into the wide world, thinking the workshop too small for his valiant deeds. Before he set out, however, he looked through his house to see if there was anything he could take with him, but he found only some old cheese, which he pocketed, and seeing a bird near the door entangled in the bushes, he caught it and put it in his pocket also. He then set out bravely on his travels, and, as he was light and active, he felt no weariness. His road led him up a hill, and when he reached the highest point of it he found a great giant sitting there, who was looking about him very composedly.

The little tailor, however, went up boldly and said, "Good day, comrade. In faith you sit there and see the whole world stretched below you. I am also on my road thither to try my luck. Would you like to go with me?"

The giant looked contemptuously at the little tailor and said, "You vagabond! You miserable fellow!"

"That may be," replied the tailor, "but here you may read what sort of man I am," and, unbuttoning his coat, he showed the giant his belt. The giant read, "SEVEN AT ONE BLOW!" and thinking they were men whom the tailor had slain, he conceived a little respect for him. Still, he wished to test him first, so, taking up a stone, he squeezed it in his hand, so that water dripped out of it. "Do that after me," said the giant, "if you have any strength."

"If it's nothing worse than that," said the tailor, "that's child's play to me." And, diving into his pocket, he brought out the cheese and squeezed it till the whey ran out of it, and he said, "Now, I think, that's a little better."

The giant did not know what to say and could not believe it of the little man. So, taking up another stone, he threw it so high that it could scarcely be seen. "There, you manikin," he said, "do that after me."

"Well done," said the tailor, "but your stone must fall down again to the ground. I will throw one up that will not come back," and, dipping into his pocket, he took out the bird and threw it into the air. The bird, rejoicing in its freedom, flew straight up and then far away and did not return. "How does that little affair please you, comrade?" asked the tailor.

"You can throw well, certainly," replied the giant. "Now let us see if you are in trim enough to carry something out of the ordinary." So saying, he led the tailor to a huge oak tree, which lay on the ground, and he said, "If you are strong enough, just help me carry this tree out of the forest."

73

"With all my heart," replied the tailor. "You take the trunk on your shoulder, and I will raise the boughs and branches that are the heaviest and carry them."

The giant took the trunk on his shoulder, but the tailor placed himself on a branch, so that the giant, who was not able to look around, was forced to carry the whole tree and the tailor besides. The tailor, being behind, was very merry and chuckled at the trick and presently began to whistle the song, "There Rode Three Tailors out at the Gate," as if carrying trees were child's play. The giant, after he had staggered along a short distance with his heavy burden, could go no farther, and shouted, "Do you hear? I must let the tree fall." The tailor, springing down, quickly embraced the tree with both arms, as if he had been carrying it, and said to the giant, "You're such a big fellow, and yet you can't carry this tree by yourself?"

Then they journeyed on farther, and when they came to a cherry tree, the giant seized the top of the tree where the ripest fruit hung, and, bending it down, gave it to the tailor to hold, telling him to eat. But the tailor was much too weak to hold the tree down, and when the giant let go, the tree flew up into the air and the tailor was carried with it. He came down on the other side, however, without injury. and the giant said, "What does that mean? Haven't you strength enough to hold that twig?" "My strength did not fail me," replied the tailor. "Do you suppose that was any challenge for one who has killed seven at one blow? I sprang over the tree because hunters were shooting below there in the thicket. Spring after me if you can." The giant made the attempt, but could not clear the tree and stuck fast in the branches, so that in this test, too, the tailor was the better man.

After this the giant said, "Since you are such a valiant fellow, come with me to our house and stay with us overnight." The tailor consented and followed him, and when they entered the cave, there sat by the fire two other giants, each with a roasted sheep in his hand, off which he was eating. The tailor sat down, thinking, "Ah, this is much more like the world than my workshop is." And soon the giant showed him a bed where he could sleep. The bed, however, was too big for him, so he slipped out of it and crept into a corner. When midnight came and the giant thought the tailor would be in a deep sleep, he got up, took a great iron bar, beat the bed through at one stroke, and supposed he had thereby given the tailor his deathblow. In the first light of dawn the giants went into the forest, quite forgetting the tailor, but presently he came up to them, quite merry. The giants were terrified, and, fearing he would kill them all, they ran away in great haste.

The tailor journeyed on, always following his nose, and after he had wandered for quite a distance, he came into the courtyard of a royal palace. As he felt rather tired, he laid himself down on the grass and went to sleep. While he lay there, people came and viewed him from all angles, and read on his belt, "SEVEN AT ONE BLOW!" "Ah," said they, "what is this great warrior doing here in time of peace? This must be some mighty hero!" So they went and told the King, thinking that, if war broke out, here was an important and useful man whom one should not part with at any price. The King took counsel and sent one of his courtiers to the tailor to ask for his fighting services, if he should be awake. The messenger stopped at the sleeper's side and waited till he stretched out his limbs and opened his eyes, and then he gave him the message. "I came here solely on that account," the tailor replied. "I am quite ready to enter the King's service." Then he was conducted away with great honor, and he was given a fine house to live in.

The courtiers, however, became jealous of the tailor and wished he were a thousand miles away. "What will happen?" they asked one another. "If we go into a battle with him, when he strikes out, seven will fall at one blow, and nothing will be left for us to do." In their rage they decided to resign, and they went all together to the King and asked his permission, saying, "We are not prepared to be associated with a man who kills seven at one blow." The King was grieved to lose all his faithful servants for the sake of one and wished that he had never seen the tailor and would have been glad to be rid of him. However, he dared not dismiss him, because he feared the tailor would kill him and all his subjects and place himself upon the throne. For a long time he deliberated, till at last he came to a decision. He sent for the tailor and told him that, as he was so great a hero, he wanted to ask a favor of him. "In a certain forest in my kingdom," said the King, "there live two giants, who, by murder, rapine, fire, and robbery, have committed great havoc, and no one dares to approach them without imperiling his own life. If you overcome and kill both these giants, I will give you my only daughter in marriage, and half my kingdom for a dowry. A hundred knights will accompany you on this mission in order to render you assistance."

"Ah, that is something for such a man as I," thought the tailor to himself. "A beautiful Princess and half a kingdom are not offered to one every day." And he replied, "Oh, yes, I will soon manage these two giants, and a hundred horsemen are not necessary for that purpose. He who kills seven at one blow need not fear two."

Thus the little tailor set out, followed by the hundred knights, to whom he said, as soon as they came to the borders of the forest, "Stay here—I would rather meet these giants alone." Then he sprang off into the forest, peering about him right and left, and after a while he saw the two giants lying asleep under a tree, snoring so loudly that the branches above them shook violently. The tailor, full of courage, filled both his pockets with stones and clambered up the tree. When he got to the middle of it he crept along a bough, so that he sat just above the sleepers, and then he let fall one stone after another on one of them. For some time the giant did not stir, but at last he awoke, pushed his companion, and said, "Why are you hitting me?"

"You are dreaming," the other giant replied. "I never hit you." They lay down again to sleep, and presently the tailor threw a stone down on the second giant. "What is that?" he exclaimed. "What are you hitting me for?"

"I did not touch you—you must be dreaming," replied the first. So they wrangled for a few minutes, but as they were both very tired from their day's work, they soon fell asleep again. Then the tailor began his sport again, and, picking out the biggest stone, he threw it with all his force on the chest of the first giant. "That's too much!" the giant exclaimed, and, springing up like a madman, he fell on his companion, who, feeling equally aggrieved, struck back. They set to in such good earnest that they rooted up trees and beat each other about until they both fell dead on the ground.

Then the tailor jumped down, saying, "How lucky it was that they did not uproot the tree I was in, or I would have had to jump on another one like a squirrel, for I am not given to flying." He drew his sword and cut a deep wound in the breast of each giant. Then he went to the horsemen and said, "The deed is done—I have given each giant his deathblow—but it was a hard job, for they uprooted trees to defend themselves with. Still, all that is useless when such a one as I comes, who killed seven at one blow."

"Are you not wounded, then?" asked they.

"That is not to be expected—they have not touched a hair of my head," replied the little man. The knights could scarcely believe him till, riding away into the forest, they found the giants lying in their blood and the uprooted trees around them.

Now the tailor demanded his promised reward of the King, but the King repented of his promise and began to think of some new scheme to get rid of the hero. "Before you receive my daughter and the half of my kingdom," said he to him, "you must perform one other heroic deed. In the forest there runs wild a unicorn, which commits great havoc and which you must first of all catch."

"I am even less afraid of a unicorn than I am of two giants! 'Seven at One Blow!—that is my motto," said the tailor. Then he took with him a rope and an ax and went to the forest, bidding those who were ordered to accompany him to wait on the outskirts. He did not have to search long, for presently the unicorn came near and prepared to rush at him as if it would pierce him on the spot. "Softly, softly!" he exclaimed. "That is not done so easily." He waited till the animal was close to him; then he sprang nimbly behind a tree. The unicorn, rushing with all its force against the tree, fixed its horn so fast in the trunk that it could not draw it out again, and so it was made prisoner. "Now I have my prisoner," said the tailor. He came from behind the tree, bound the rope around the unicorn's neck, and then cut the horn out of the tree with his ax. He put all in order and led the animal before the King.

The King, however, would not yet deliver the promised reward. He made a third request—that before the wedding the tailor should catch a wild boar which did much injury, and he should have the huntsmen to help him. "With pleasure," the tailor replied. "It is mere child's play." The huntsmen, however, he left behind. They were entirely content with the arrangement, for this wild boar had hunted them so often that they had no desire to hunt it. As soon as the boar saw the tailor, it ran at him with gaping mouth and glistening teeth and tried to throw him to the ground, but our flying hero sprang into a little chapel nearby, then sprang out again through a window on the other side. The boar ran after him, but the tailor, skipping around, shut the door behind it, and there the raging beast was caught, for it was much too heavy to jump out the window. The tailor now called the huntsmen, so they might see his prisoner with their own eyes. The tailor then presented himself before the King, who was now compelled, whether he wanted to or not, to keep his promise and surrender his daughter and half his kingdom.

If he had known that it was no warrior but only a tailor who stood before him, he would have been even more stricken!

So the wedding was celebrated with great splendor, though with little rejoicing, and out of a tailor was made a King.

Some little while afterward the young Queen heard her husband talking in his sleep, saying, "Boy, make me a waistcoat and

stitch up these trousers, or I will box your ears with the yard measure!" Then she realized what her lord was and complained in the morning to her father and begged him to deliver her from her husband, who was nothing but a tailor. The King comforted her by saying, "This night leave your chamber door open; my servants will stand without, and when he is asleep they will enter, bind him, and take him to a ship, which will carry him forth into the wide world." The wife was contented with his proposal, but the King's armor bearer, who had overheard it all, went to the husband and disclosed the whole plot. "I will settle this matter," said the brave tailor. In the evening at their usual time they went to bed, and when his wife thought he was asleep, she got up, opened the door, then went back to bed. The tailor, however, only pretended to be asleep, and he began to exclaim in a loud voice, "Boy, make me a waistcoat and stitch up these trousers, or I will box your ears with the yard measure! Seven have I killed with one blow, two giants have I slain, a unicorn have I captured, and a wild boar have I caught, and shall I be afraid of those who stand outside my chamber?" When the men heard these words spoken by the tailor, a great fear overcame them, and they ran away as if the wild huntsmen were behind them; neither did any man after that dare venture to oppose him. Thus the tailor became a King, and so he remained the rest of his days.

THE SIX SWANS

NDER the great trees of the forest a King pursued his game so hotly that none of his courtiers could follow him. When evening approached, the King stopped and, looking around him, perceived that he had become lost. He sought a path out of the forest but could not find one, and presently he saw an old woman, her head nodding, coming toward him. "My good woman," said the King, "can you show me the way out of the forest?"

"Oh, yes, my lord King," she replied. "I can do that very well, but on one condition, and if you do not fulfill it, you will never again get out of the wood, but will die of hunger."

"What is this condition?" asked the King.

"I have a daughter," said the old woman, "who is as beautiful as anyone you can find in the whole world, and well deserves to be your bride. Now, if you will make her your Queen, I will show you your way out of the wood." In his anxiety the King consented, and the old woman led him to her cottage, where the daughter was sitting by the fire. She received the King as if she had expected him, and he saw at once that she was very beautiful, yet she did not quite please him, for he could not look at her without a secret shuddering. However, he took the maiden on his horse, and the old woman showed him the way, and the King arrived safely at his palace, where the wedding was to be celebrated.

The King had been married once before and had seven children by his first wife, six boys and a girl, whom he loved more than everything else in the world. He soon became afraid that the stepmother might not treat them very well and might even do them some great injury, so he took them away to a lonely castle that stood in the midst of a forest. This castle was so hidden and the way to it so difficult to discover that he himself could not have found it if a wise woman had not given him a ball of cotton which had the wonderful property, when he threw it before him, of unrolling itself and showing him the right path. However, the King went so often to see his dear children that the Queen noticed his absence, became inquisitive, and wanted to know what he went to get in the forest. So she gave his servants a great quantity of money, and they disclosed to her the secret, and also told her of the ball of cotton which alone could show her the way. She now had no peace until she discovered where this ball was concealed, and then she made some fine silk shirts, and, as she had learned from her mother, she sewed into each one a charm. One day soon after, when the King was out hunting, she took the little shirts and went into the forest, and the cotton showed her the path. The six boys, seeing someone coming in the distance, thought it was their dear father and ran out toward her, full of joy. Then she threw over each of them a shirt, which, as it touched their bodies, changed them into swans, which flew away over the forest. The Queen then went home quite contented and thought she was free of her stepchildren, but the little girl had not gone with her brothers to meet her, and the Queen did not know she existed.

The following day the King went to visit his children, but he found only the girl. "Where are your brothers?" he asked. "Ah, dear father," she replied, "they have gone away and left me alone." She told him how she had looked out of the window and had seen them changed into swans, which had flown over the forest, and then she showed him the feathers which they had dropped in the court-yard and which she had collected. The King was deeply grieved, but he did not think that his wife could have done this wicked deed, and, as he feared the girl might also be stolen away, he took her with him. She was, however, so afraid of her stepmother that she begged him not to make her stay more than one night in the castle.

The poor maiden thought to herself, "This is no longer my place—I will go and look for my brothers," and when night came she escaped and went quite deep into the wood. She walked all night long and a great part of the next day, until she was so weary she could go no farther. Just then she saw a rude hut, and when she walked in she found a room with six little beds. She dared not get into one, but crept underneath and, laying herself upon the hard dirt floor, prepared to spend the night there. Just as the sun was set-ting, she heard a rustling and saw six white swans come flying in at the window. They settled on the floor and began blowing on one another until they had blown all their feathers off, and their swans-down stripped off like a shirt. The maiden knew at once that they were her brothers, and she gladly crept out from under the bed. The brothers were no less glad to see their sister, but their joy was of short duration. "You must not stay here," they said to her. "This is a robbers' hiding place; if they returned and found you here, they would murder you." "Can't you protect me, then?" inquired the sister.

"No," one of them replied, "for we can lay aside our swan's feathers for only a quarter of an hour each evening. For that time we regain our human form, but afterwards we resume our changed appearance."

Their sister then asked tearfully, "Can't you be restored again?"

"Oh, no," he replied, "the conditions are too difficult. For six long years you must neither speak nor laugh, and during that time you must sew for us six little shirts of starflowers, and if a single word falls from your lips, then all your labor will be in vain." Just as the brother finished speaking, the quarter of an hour elapsed, and they flew out the window again like swans.

The little sister, however, made a solemn resolution to rescue her brothers or die in the attempt. She left the cottage and, penetrating deep into the forest, passed the night perched amid the branches of a tree. The next morning she went out and collected the starflowers to sew together. She had no one to converse with and no heart for laughing, so she sat there in the tree, intent on her work. After she had passed some time there, it happened that the King of that country was hunting in the forest, and his huntsmen stopped under the tree in which the maiden sat. They called to her and asked, "Who are you?" but she did not answer. "Come down to us," they continued. "We will do you no harm." She merely shook her head, and when they pressed her further with questions, she threw down to them her gold necklace, hoping therewith to satisfy them. They did not, however, leave her, and she threw down her belt, but to no avail, and even her beautiful dress did not make them desist. At last one of the huntsmen climbed the tree, carried down the maiden, and took her before the King. The King asked her, "Who are you? What do you do up in the tree?" But she did not answer, and then he asked her in all the languages that he knew, but she remained as dumb as a fish. Since, however, she was so beautiful, the King's heart was touched, and he developed a strong affection for her. Then he put his cloak around her, placed her in front of him on the saddle on his horse, and took her to his castle. There he ordered rich clothing to be made for her, and, although her beauty shone as the sunbeams, not a word escaped her. The King placed her by his side at the table during meals, and there her dignified mien and manners so charmed him that he said, "This maiden will I marry, and no other in the world," and after some days he was united to her.

Now, the King had a wicked stepmother, who was displeased with his marriage and spoke evil of the young Queen. "Who knows where the wench comes from?" she said. "She who cannot speak is not worthy of a King." A year after, when the young Queen brought her firstborn into the world, the King's stepmother took him away. Then she went to the King and complained that the Queen was a murderess. The King, however, would not believe it and would allow no one to speak ill of his wife, who sat composedly sewing on her shirts and paying attention to nothing else. When a second child was born, the evil stepmother stole that child, too, and again accused the Queen, but the King would not listen to her, but said, "She is too pious and good to act so. If she could speak and defend herself, her innocence would be apparent." But when again, the third time, the old woman stole the child and then accused the Queen, who answered not a word in her own defense, the King was obliged to order a trial, and she was condemned to death by fire.

When the sentence was due to be carried out, it happened to be the very day when her dear brothers would be freed; the six shirts were ready, all but the last, which still needed the left sleeve sewed in. As she was led to the scaffold, she carried the shirts in her arms, and just as the fire was about to be kindled, she looked around and saw six swans come flying through the air. Her heart leaped with joy as she saw her deliverers approaching, and soon the swans, flying toward her, alighted so near that she was able to throw the shirts over them, and as soon as she had done so, their feathers fell off and the brothers stood up alive and well, but the youngest had, instead of a left arm, a swan's wing. The brothers embraced and kissed the

Queen. The Queen went to the King, who was thunderstruck. "Now may I speak, my dear husband," she said, "and prove to you that I am innocent and falsely accused." And then she told him how the wicked woman had stolen away and hidden her three children. When she had finished, the King was overcome with joy. The children were brought safely back, and the wicked stepmother was led to the scaffold and bound to the stake and burned to ashes.

The King and the Queen forever after lived in peace and prosperity with the children and the six brothers.

THE JUNIPER TREE

 ERY long ago, perhaps as much as two thousand years ago, there was a rich man who had a wife of whom he was very fond, but they had no children. Now in the garden, before the house where they lived, there stood a juniper tree, and one winter's day as the lady was standing under the juniper tree, paring an apple, she cut her finger, and the drops of blood trickled down on the snow. "Ah," said she, sighing deeply and looking down at the blood, "how happy I would be if I had a little child as white as snow and as red as blood!" And as she was saying this, she grew quite cheerful and was sure her wish would be fulfilled. And after a little time the snow went away, and soon afterward the

fields began to look green. Next the spring came, and the meadows were dressed with flowers; the trees put forth their green leaves; the young branches shed their blossoms on the ground, and the little birds sang through the groves. And then came summer, and the sweet-smelling flowers of the juniper tree began to unfold, and the lady's heart leaped within her, and she fell on her knees for joy. But when autumn drew near, the fruit was thick upon the trees. Then the lady plucked the berries from the juniper tree, and looked sad and sorrowful, and she called her husband to her and said, "If I die, bury me under the juniper tree." Not long after this a pretty little child was born; it was, as the lady wished, as red as blood and as white as snow, and as soon as she had looked upon it, her joy overcame her, and she fainted away and died.

Then her husband buried her under the juniper tree and wept and mourned over her, but after a little while he grew better and at length dried his tears and married another wife.

Time passed, and a daughter was born, but the child of his first wife, that was as red as blood and as white as snow, was a little boy. The mother loved her daughter very much, but hated the little boy, and wondered how she could get all her husband's money for her own child. She treated the poor fellow very harshly, and was always pushing him from one corner of the house to another, and thumping him and pinching him, so that he was forever in fear of her, and when he came home from school he could never find a place in the house to play in.

Now it happened that once when the mother was going into her storeroom, the little girl came to her and asked, "Mother, may I have an apple?" "Yes, my dear," said the mother, and gave her a nice rosy apple out of the chest. The chest had a thick heavy lid, with a great sharp iron lock on it. "Mother," said the little girl, "pray give me one for my little brother, too." Her mother did not like this very much, but she said, "Yes, my child, when he comes from school, he will have one too." As she spoke, she looked out the window and saw the little boy coming, so she took the apple from her daughter and threw it back into the chest and shut the lid, telling her that she could have it again when her brother came home. When the little boy came to the door, the wicked woman said to him in a kind voice, "Come in, my dear, and I will give you an apple." "How kind you are, Mother!" said the little boy. "I'd like to have an apple very much." "Well, come with me then," said she. So she took him into the storeroom and lifted the cover of the chest and said, "There, take one out yourself," and then as the little boy stooped down to take one of the apples out of the chest, *bang!* she let the lid fall so hard that his head fell off among the apples. When she realized what she had done, she was very frightened and did not know how she should get the blame off her shoulders. However, she went into her bedroom and took a white handkerchief out of a drawer and then fitted the little boy's head on his neck and tied the handkerchief around it, so that no one could see what had happened, and seated him on a stool before the door with the apple in his hand.

Soon afterward Margery came into the kitchen to her mother, who was standing by the fire and stirring some soup in a pot. "Mother," said Margery, "my brother is sitting before the door with an apple in his hand. I asked him to give it to me, but he didn't say a word, and he looked so pale that I was quite frightened." "Nonsense!" said her mother. "Go back, and if he won't answer you, give him a good box on the ear." Margery went back and said, "Brother, give me that apple." But he answered not a word, so she gave him a box on the ear, and immediately his head fell off. At this she was sadly frightened and ran screaming out to her mother that she had knocked off her brother's head, and cried as if her heart would break. "Oh, Margery!" said her mother. "What have you been doing? However, what is done can't be undone, so we had better put him out of the way and say nothing to anyone about it."

When the father came home to dinner, he said, "Where is my little boy?" And his wife said nothing, but put a large bowl of black soup on the table, and Margery wept bitterly all the time and could not hold up her head. And the father asked after his little boy again. "Oh!" said his wife. "I think he has gone to his uncle's." "Why would he go away without saying good-bye to me?" said his father. "I know he wanted very much to go," said the woman, "and he begged me to let him stay there for some time. He will be well taken care of there." "Ah," said the father, "I don't like that. He shouldn't have gone away without saying good-bye to me." And with that he began to eat, but he still seemed sorrowful about his son, and he said, "Margery, why are you crying so? Your brother will come back again, I hope." But Margery slipped out of the room and went to her bureau and took out her best handkerchief and tied it around her little brother's bones. She carried them out of the house, weeping bitterly all the while, and laid them under the juniper tree. As soon as she had done this, her heart felt lighter, and she stopped crying. Then the juniper tree began to move backwards and forwards and to stretch its branches out, one from another, and then bring them together again, just like a person clapping hands for joy, and after this a kind of cloud came from the tree, and in the middle of the cloud was a burning fire, and out of the fire came a pretty bird that flew away into the air, singing merrily. And as soon as the bird was gone, the handkerchief and the little boy were gone too, and the tree looked just as it had before, but Margery felt quite happy and joyful within herself, just as if she knew that her brother was alive again, and she went into the house and ate her dinner.

But the bird flew away and perched on the roof of a goldsmith's house and sang:

> *"My mother slew her little son,*
> *My father thought me lost and gone,*
> *But pretty Margery pitied me,*
> *And laid me under the juniper tree,*
> *And now I rove so merrily,*
> *As over the hills and dales I fly.*
> *O what a fine bird am I!"*

The goldsmith was sitting in his shop, finishing a gold chain, and when he heard the bird singing on the housetop, he started up so suddenly that one of his shoes slipped off. However, without stopping to put it on again, he ran out into the street with his apron on, holding his pincers in one hand and the gold chain in the other. And when he saw the bird sitting on the roof with the sun shining on its bright feathers, he said, "How sweetly you sing, my pretty bird! Pray sing that song again." "No," said the bird, "I can't sing twice for nothing. If you will give me that gold chain, I'll see what I can do." "There," said the goldsmith, "take the chain, only please sing that song again." So the bird flew down, and taking the chain in his right claw, perched a little nearer to the goldsmith, and sang:

"My mother slew her little son,
My father thought me lost and gone,
But pretty Margery pitied me,
And laid me under the juniper tree,
And now I rove so merrily,
As over the hills and dales I fly.
O what a fine bird am I!"

After that the bird flew away to a shoemaker's and, sitting on the roof of the house, sang the same song as it had done before.

When the shoemaker heard the song, he ran to the door without his coat and looked up at the top of the house, but he was obliged to hold his hand before his eyes, because the sun shone so brightly. "Bird," said he, "how sweetly you sing!" Then he called into the house. "Wife! Wife! come out here and see what a pretty bird is singing on the top of our house!" And he called out his children and workmen, and they all ran out and stood gazing at the bird, with its beautiful red and green feathers, and the bright golden ring around its neck, and eyes that glittered like the stars. "O bird," said the shoemaker, "pray sing that song again." "No," said the bird, "I cannot sing twice for nothing. You must give me something if I do." "Wife," said the shoemaker, "run upstairs into the workshop and bring me down the best pair of new red shoes you can find." So his wife ran and fetched them. "Here, my pretty bird," said the shoe-maker, "take these shoes, but please sing that song again." The bird came down and, taking the shoes in his left claw, flew up again to the housetop and sang:

> *"My mother slew her little son,*
> *My father thought me lost and gone,*
> *But pretty Margery pitied me,*
> *And laid me under the juniper tree,*
> *And now I rove so merrily,*
> *As over the hills and dales I fly.*
> *O what a fine bird am I!"*

And when he had done singing, he flew away, holding the shoes in one claw and the chain in the other. And he flew a long, long way off, till at last he came to a mill. The mill was going *clipper! clapper! clipper! clapper!*, and in the mill were twenty millers, who were all hard at work hewing a millstone, and the millers hewed *hick! hack! hick! hack!* and the mill went on, *clipper! clapper! clipper! clapper!*

So the bird perched on a linden tree close by the mill and began its song:

> *"My mother slew her little son,*
> *My father thought me lost and gone."*

Here two of the millers left off their work and listened:

> *"But pretty Margery pitied me,*
> *And laid me under the juniper tree."*

Now all the millers but one looked up and left their work.

> *"And now I rove so merrily,*

95

As over the hills and dales I fly.
O what a fine bird am I!"

Just as the song was ended, the last miller heard it and started up and said, "O bird! How sweetly you sing! Do let me hear the whole of that song. Pray, sing it again!" "No," said the bird, "I cannot sing twice for nothing. Give me that millstone, and I'll sing again." "Why," said the man, "the millstone does not belong to me. If it were all mine, you could have it and welcome." "Come," said the other millers, "if he will sing that song again, he can have the millstone." Then the bird came down from the tree, and the twenty millers got long poles and worked and worked—heave, ho! heave, ho!—till at last they raised the millstone on its side, and then the bird put its head through the hole in the middle of it, and flew away to the linden tree, and sang the same song it had sung before.

And when he had done, he spread his wings, and with the chain in one claw, and the shoes in the other, and the millstone around his neck, he flew away to his father's house.

Now it happened that his father and mother and Margery were sitting together at dinner. His father was saying, "How light and cheerful I am!" But his mother said, "Oh, I am so heavy and so sad, I feel just as if a great storm were coming on." And Margery said nothing, but sat and cried. Just then the bird came flying along and perched on the top of the house. "Bless me!" said the father. "How cheerful I am—I feel as if I were about to see an old friend again." "Alas!" said the mother. "I am so sad, and my teeth chatter so, and yet it seems as if my blood were all on fire in my veins!" and she tore open her gown to cool herself. And Margery sat by herself in a corner, with her plate on her lap before her, and wept so bitterly that she cried her plate quite full of tears.

And the bird flew to the top of the juniper tree and sang:

"My mother slew her little son . . ."

Then the mother held her ears with her hands, and shut her eyes, so that she might neither see nor hear, but there was a sound in her ears like a frightful storm, and her eyes burned and glared like lightning.

> *"My father thought me lost and gone . . ."*

"O wife!" said the father. "What a beautiful bird that is, and how finely he sings, and his feathers glitter in the sun like so many spangles!"

> *"But pretty Margery pitied me,*
> *And laid me under the juniper tree . . ."*

At this Margery lifted her head and sobbed sadly, and her father said, "I must go out and look at that bird a little nearer." "Oh, don't leave me alone," said his wife. "I feel just as if the house were burning." However, he did go out to look at the bird, and it went on singing:

> *"And now I rove so merrily,*
> *As over the hills and dales I fly.*
> *O what a fine bird am I!"*

As soon as the bird had finished singing, he let fall the gold chain on his father's neck, and it fitted so nicely that the father went back into the house and said, "Look here, what a beautiful chain the bird has given me—see how grand it is!" But his wife was so frightened that she fell on the floor, so that her cap flew off and she lay as if she were dead. And when the bird began singing again, Margery said, "I must go out and see whether the bird has not something to give me." And just as she was going out the door, the bird let fall the red shoes before her, and when she had put on the shoes, she all at once became quite light and happy and jumped into the house and said, "I was so heavy and sad when I went out, and now I'm so happy! See what fine shoes the bird has given me!" Then the mother said, "Well, even if the world falls to pieces, I must go out and see whether I shall not be better in the air." And as she was going out, the bird let fall the millstone on her head and crushed her to pieces.

The father and Margery, hearing the noise, ran out and saw nothing but smoke and fire and flame rising from the place, and when this was passed and gone, there stood the little boy beside them, and he took his father and Margery by the hand, and they went into the house and ate their dinner together very happily.

THE TWO BROTHERS

LONG time ago there were two brothers, one rich and the other poor. The rich man was a goldsmith and of an evil disposition; the poor brother maintained himself by mending brooms, and withal was honest and pious. He had two children—twins, as like one another as two drops of water—who often went to their rich uncle's house and received a meal off the fragments which he left. One day it happened when the poor man had gone into the wood for twigs that he saw a bird, which was of gold and more beautiful than any he had ever before set eyes on. He picked up a stone and flung it at the bird, and hit it, but so slightly that only a single feather dropped off. This feather

99

he took to his brother, who looked at it and said, "It is of pure gold!" and gave him a good sum of money for it. The next day he climbed a birch tree to lop off a bough or two, and the same bird flew out of the branches, and as the man looked around he found a nest which contained an egg, also of gold. This he took home, as before, to his brother, who said it was of pure gold, and who gave him what it was worth, but said that he must have the bird itself. For the third time the brother went into the forest and saw the golden bird sitting again on the tree, and he took up a stone and threw it at it, and, securing it, took it to his brother, who gave him a large pile of gold for it. With this the man went home lighthearted.

But the goldsmith was crafty and bold, knowing very well what sort of bird it was. He called his wife and said to her, "Roast this bird for me, and take care of whatever falls from it, for I have a mind to eat it by myself." Now, the bird was certainly not an ordinary one, for it possessed this wonderful power, that whoever ate its heart and liver would find henceforth every morning a gold piece under his pillow. The wife made the bird ready and, putting it on a spit, set it down to roast. Now it happened that while it was at the fire, and the woman had gone out of the kitchen on some other necessary work, the two children of the poor broom mender ran in and began to turn the spit around at the fire for amusement. Presently two little tidbits fell down into the pan out of the bird, and one of the boys said, "Let us eat these two little pieces. I am so hungry, and nobody will find it out." So they quickly ate the two morsels, and presently the woman came back, and, seeing at once that they had eaten something, asked them what it was. "Two little bits that fell down out of the bird," was the reply. "They were the heart and liver!" exclaimed the woman, quite frightened, and in order that her husband might not miss them and be in a fury, she quickly killed a little chicken, took out its liver and heart, and put them inside the golden bird. As soon as the bird was done enough, she carried it to the goldsmith, who devoured it quite alone and left nothing at all on his plate. The next morning, however, when he looked under his pillow, expecting to find a gold piece, there was not the smallest one to be seen.

The two children did not know what good luck had fallen upon them, and, when they got up the next morning, something fell ringing on the floor, and when they picked it up they found it was two gold pieces. They took them to their father, who wondered very much about it, and considered what he should do with them, but as the next morning the same thing happened, and so on every day, he went to his brother and told him the whole story. The goldsmith perceived at once what had happened—that the children had eaten the heart and the liver of his bird—and in order to revenge himself, and because he was so covetous and hardhearted, he persuaded the father that his children were in league with the devil, and warned him not to take the gold, but to turn them out of the house, for the Evil One had them in his power and would make them do some mischief. Their father feared the Evil One, and, although it cost him a severe pang, he led his children out in the forest and left them there with a sad heart.

Now, the two children ran through the wood, seeking the road home, but could not find it, so that they only wandered farther away. At last they met a huntsman, who asked to whom they belonged. "We are the children of the poor broom mender," they replied, and told him that their father could no longer keep them at home, because a gold piece lay under their pillows every morning. "Well," replied the huntsman, "that does not seem right, if you are honest and not idle." And the good man, having no children of his own, took the twins home with him, because they pleased him, and he told them he would be their father and bring them up. With him they learned all kinds of hunting, and the gold pieces, which each one found every morning, they laid aside against a rainy day.

When they became young men, the huntsman took them into the forest and said, "Today you must perform your shooting trial, so that I may make you free huntsmen like me." So they went with him and waited a long time, but no wild beast approached. The huntsman, looking up, saw a flock of wild geese flying overhead in the form of a triangle. "Shoot one from each corner," said he to the twins, and when they had done this, another flock came flying over in the form of a figure two, and from these they were also told to shoot one at each corner. When they had performed this deed successfully, their foster father said, "I now make you free, for you are excellent marksmen."

Thereupon the two brothers went together into the forest, laying plans and consulting with each other, and when that evening they sat down to their meal, they said to their foster father, "We shall not touch the least morsel of food till you have granted our request."

He asked them what it was, and they replied, "We have now learned everything. Let us go into the world and see what we can do there, and let us set out at once."

"You have spoken like brave huntsmen," cried the old man, overjoyed. "What you have asked is just what I wished. You can set out as soon as you like, for you will be prosperous."

Then they ate and drank together once more with great joy and hilarity.

When the appointed day arrived, the old huntsman gave each youth a good rifle and a dog and let them take from the gold pieces as many as they liked. Then he accompanied them part of their way, and on leaving, gave them a bare knife, saying, "If you should separate, stick this knife in a tree by the roadside, and then, if one returns to the same point, he can tell how his absent brother fares, for the side on which there is a mark will, if he dies, rust, but as long as he lives it will be as bright as ever."

The two brothers now journeyed on till they came to a forest so large that they could not possibly get out of it in one day, so there they passed the night and ate what they had in their hunters' pockets. The second day they still walked on, but came to no opening, and having nothing to eat, one said, "We must shoot something, or we shall die of hunger," and he loaded his gun and looked around. Just then an old hare came running up. The brother aimed at it, but it cried out:

> *"Dear huntsman, pray now let me live,*
> *And I will two young leverets give."*

So saying, it ran back into the brush and brought out two hares, but they played about so prettily and actively that the hunters could not make up their minds to kill them. So they took them with them, and the two leverets followed in their footsteps. Presently a fox came up to them, and as they were about to shoot it, it cried out:

> *"Dear hunters, pray now let me live,*
> *And I will two young foxes give."*

These the fox brought them, and the brothers, instead of killing them, put them with the young hares, and all four followed. In a little while a wolf came out of the brush. The hunters also aimed at him, but he cried out as the others had:

> *"Dear hunters, pray now let me live.*
> *Two young ones, in return, I'll give."*

The hunters placed the two wolves with the other animals, who still followed them, and soon they met a bear, who also begged for his life, saying:

> *"Dear hunters, pray now let me live.*
> *Two young ones, in return, I'll give."*

These two bears were added to the others; they made eight; and now who came last? A lion, shaking his mane. The two brothers were not frightened; they aimed at him, and he cried:

> *"Dear hunters, pray now let me live.*
> *Two young ones, in return, I'll give."*

The lion then fetched his two young cubs, and now the huntsmen had two lions, two bears, two wolves, two foxes, and two hares following and waiting on them. Meanwhile their hunger had received no satisfaction, and they said to the foxes, "Here, you slinks, get us something to eat, for you are both sly and crafty."

The foxes replied, "Not far from here lies a village where we can procure many fowls, and we will show you the way there."

So they went into the village and bought something to eat for themselves and their animals, and then went on farther, for the foxes were well acquainted with the country where the hen roosts were, and so could direct the huntsmen well.

For some little way they walked on without finding any situations where they could live together, so they said to one another, "It cannot be otherwise—we must separate." Then the two brothers divided the beasts, so that each one had a lion, a bear, a wolf, a fox, and a hare, and then they took leave of each other, promising to love each other till death, and the knife their foster father had given them they stuck in a tree, so that one side pointed to the east and the other to the west.

One brother came with his animals to a town that was completely hung with black crape. He went into an inn and inquired if he could lodge his beasts, and the landlord gave him a stable, and in the wall was a hole through which the hare crept and seized upon a cabbage; the fox fetched himself a hen, and when he had eaten it he stole the cock also, but the lion, the bear, and the wolf, being too big for the hole, could get nothing. The master, therefore, made the host fetch an ox for them, on which they feasted merrily, and so, having seen after his beasts, he asked the landlord why the town was all hung in mourning. The landlord replied that it was because the next day the King's only daughter was to die. "Is she then sick unto death?" inquired the huntsman.

"No," replied the other, "she is well enough, but still she must die."`

"How is that?" asked the huntsman.

"Out there before the town," said the landlord, "is a high

mountain on which lives a dragon, who every year must have a pure maiden, or he would lay waste all the country. Now, all the maidens have been given up, and there is only one left, the King's daughter, who must also be given up, for there is no escape, and tomorrow morning it is to happen."

The huntsman asked, "Why is the dragon not killed?"

"Ah!" replied the landlord. "Many knights have tried, but every one has lost his life, and the King has promised his own daughter to him who conquers the dragon, and after his death the inheritance of his kingdom."

The huntsman said nothing further at that time, but the next morning, taking with him his beasts, he climbed the dragon's mountain. A little way up stood a chapel, and on an altar therein were three cups, and by them was written, "Whoever drinks the contents of these cups will be the strongest man on earth, and may take the sword that lies buried beneath the threshold." Without drinking, the huntsman sought and found the sword in the ground, but he could not move it from its place, so he entered, and drank out of the cups, and then he easily pulled out the sword and was so strong that he waved it about like a feather.

When the hour arrived that the maiden should be delivered over to the dragon, the King and his Marshal accompanied her with all the court. From a distance they perceived the huntsman on the mountain, and took him for the dragon waiting for them, and so would not ascend, but at last, because the whole city would otherwise have been sacrificed, the Princess was forced to make the dreadful ascent. The King and his courtiers returned home full of grief, but the Marshal had to stop and watch it all from a distance.

As the King's daughter reached the top of the hill, she found there not the dragon but the young hunter, who comforted her, saying he would save her. He led her into the chapel and shut her up therein. In a short time the seven-headed dragon came roaring up with a tremendous noise, and as soon as he perceived the hunter, he asked, amazed, "What are you doing on my mountain?"

The hunter replied that he had come to fight him, and the dragon said, breathing out fire as he spoke from his seven jaws, "Many a knight has already left his life behind him, and you I will soon kill as dead as they." The fire from his throat set the grass in a blaze and would have suffocated the hunter with the smoke if his beasts had not come running up and stamped it out. Then the dragon made a dart at the hunter, but the hunter swung his sword around so that it whistled in the air and cut off three of the beast's heads. The dragon now became furious and raised himself in the air, spitting out fire over his enemy and trying to overthrow him, but the hunter, springing on one side, raised his sword again and cut off three more of his heads. The beast was half killed with this and sank down, but tried once more to catch the hunter. The hunter beat him off and, with his last strength, cut off his tail, and then, being unable to fight any longer, he called his beasts, who came and tore the dragon in pieces.

As soon as the battle was over, he went to the chapel and unlocked the door and found the Princess lying on the floor, for, from anguish and terror, she had fainted while the contest was going on. The hunter carried her out, and when she came to herself and opened her eyes, he showed her the dragon torn to pieces and said she was now safe forever. The sight made her quite happy, and she said, "Now you will be my husband, for my father has promised me to him who should kill the dragon." So saying, she took off her necklace of coral and divided it among the beasts for a reward, the lion receiving the gold clasp for his share. But her handkerchief, on which her name was embroidered, she presented to the huntsman, who went and cut out the tongues of the dragon's seven mouths, and, wrapping them in the handkerchief, preserved them carefully.

All this being done, the poor fellow felt so weary after the battle with the dragon and the fire that he said to the Princess, "Since we are both so tired, let us sleep awhile." She consented, and they lay down on the ground, and the hunter bid the lion watch that nobody surprised them. Soon they began to snore, and the lion

sat down near them to watch, but he was also weary with fighting, and he said to the bear, "Do lie down near me, for I must sleep a bit, but wake me up if anyone comes." So the bear did as he was told, but as he soon got tired, he asked the wolf to watch for him. The wolf consented, but before long he called the fox and said, "Do watch for me a little while. I want to have a nap, and you can wake me if anyone comes." The fox lay down by his side, but soon felt so tired himself that he called the hare and asked him to take his place and watch while he slept a little. The hare came and, lying down too, soon felt very sleepy, but he had no one to call in his place, so by degrees he dropped off himself and began to snore. Here, then, were sleeping the Princess, the huntsman, the lion, the bear, the wolf, the fox, and the hare, and all were very sound asleep.

Meanwhile the Marshal, who had been set to watch below, not seeing the dragon fly away with the Princess, and all appearing very quiet, took heart and climbed the mountain. There lay the dragon, dead and torn to pieces on the ground, and not far off the King's daughter and a huntsman with his beasts, all reposing in a deep sleep. Now, the Marshal was very wickedly disposed, and, taking his sword, he cut off the head of the huntsman, and then, taking the maiden under his arm, carried her down the mountain. At this she awoke, terrified, and the Marshal cried to her, "You are in my hands; you must say that it was I who killed the dragon."

"That I cannot," she replied, "for a hunter and his animals did it." Then he drew his sword and threatened her with death if she did not obey, till at last she was forced to consent. Thereupon he brought her before the King, who was almost beside himself with joy at seeing again his dear daughter, who, he had supposed, had been torn in pieces by the monster. The Marshal told the King that he had killed the dragon and had freed the Princess and the whole kingdom, and therefore he demanded her for a wife, as had been promised. The King inquired of his daughter if it was true. "Ah, yes," she replied, "it must be so, but I make a condition, that the wedding shall not take place for a year and a day," for she thought to herself that perhaps in that time she might hear some news of her dear huntsman.

But up on the dragon's mountain the animals still lay asleep beside their dead master. Presently a great bee came and settled on the hare's nose, but he lifted his paw and brushed it off. The bee came a second time, but the hare brushed it off again and went to sleep. For the third time the bee settled and stung the hare's nose so that he woke up completely. As soon as he had risen and shaken himself, he awoke the fox, and the fox awoke the wolf, the wolf awoke the bear, and the bear awoke the lion. As soon as the lion got up and saw that the maiden was gone and his dear master was dead, he began to roar fearfully and asked, "Who has done this? Bear, why did you not wake me?" The bear asked the wolf, "Why did you not wake me?" The wolf asked the fox, "Why did you not wake me?" and the fox asked the hare, "Why did you not wake me?" The poor hare alone had nothing to answer, and the blame was attached to him, and the others would have fallen upon him, but he begged for his life, saying, "Do not kill me, and I will restore our dear master to life. I know a hill where grows a root, and he who puts it in his mouth is healed immediately from all diseases or wounds, but this mountain lies two hundred hours' journey from here."

The lion said, "In four-and-twenty hours you must go and return here, bringing the root with you."

The hare immediately ran off, and in four-and-twenty hours returned with the root in his mouth. Now the lion put the huntsman's head again to his body while the hare applied the root to the wound, and immediately the huntsman began to revive, and his heartbeat and life returned. The huntsman now awoke and was frightened to see the maiden no longer with him, and he thought to himself, "Perhaps she ran away while I slept, to get rid of me." In his haste the lion had unluckily set his master's head on the wrong way, but the hunter did not find it out till midday, when he wanted to eat, being so occupied with thinking about the Princess. Then, when he wished to help himself, he discovered his head was turned to his back, and, unable to imagine the cause, he asked the animals what had happened to him in his sleep. The lion told him that from weariness they had all gone to sleep, and, on awaking, they had found him dead, with his head cut off; that the hare had fetched the life root, but in his great haste he had turned his head the wrong way, but that he would make it all right again in no time. So saying, he cut off the huntsman's head and turned it around, while the hare healed the wound with the root.

After this the hunter became very listless and went about from place to place, letting his animals dance before the people for show. It chanced, after a year's time, that he came again into the same town where he had rescued the Princess from the dragon, and this time the town was hung everywhere with scarlet cloth. He asked the landlord of the inn, "What does this mean? A year ago the city was hung with black crape, and today it's all in red!" The landlord replied, "A year ago our King's daughter was delivered to the dragon, but our Marshal fought with it and slew it, and this day their marriage is to be celebrated. Before, the town was hung with crape as a token of our grief and lamentation, but today it's hung with scarlet cloth to show our joy."

The next day, when the wedding was to take place, the huntsman said to the landlord, "Believe it or not, my host, today I will eat bread from the table of the King!"

"Well," said the landlord, "I will wager you a hundred pieces of gold that that doesn't come true."

The huntsman accepted the bet and laid down his money. Then he called the hare and said, "Go, dear Jumper, and fetch me a bit of bread such as the King eats."

Now, the hare was the smallest and therefore could not entrust his business to anyone else, but was obliged to make himself ready to go. "Oh," thought he, "if I jump along the streets alone, the butcher's dogs will come out after me."

While he stood considering, it happened as he thought, for the dogs came behind and were about to seize him for a choice morsel, but he made a spring (had you but seen it!) and escaped into a sentry box without the soldier's knowing it. The dogs came and tried to hunt him out, but the soldier, not understanding what they were after, beat them off with a club, so that they ran howling and barking away. As soon as the hare saw that the coast was clear, he ran up to the castle and into the room where the Princess was and, getting under her stool, began to scratch her foot. The Princess said, "Will you be quiet?", thinking it was her dog. Then the hare scratched her foot a second time, and she said again, "Will you be quiet?" But the hare would not stop, and a third time scratched her foot, and now she peeped down and recognized the hare by his necklace. She took him up in her arms and carried him into her chamber. "Dear hare, what do you want?" The hare replied, "My master who killed the dragon is here and sent me. I have come for a piece of bread such as the King eats."

At these words she became very glad and bade her servant bring her a piece of bread such as the King was accustomed to have. When it was brought, the hare said, "The baker must carry it for me, or the butcher's dogs will seize it." So the baker carried it to the door of the inn, where the hare got up on his hind legs and, taking the bread in his forepaws, carried it to his master. Then the huntsman said, "See here, my host, the hundred gold pieces are mine."

The landlord wondered very much, but the huntsman said further, "Yes, I have got the King's bread, and now I will have some of his meat." To this the landlord demurred, but would not bet again, and his guest, calling the fox, said, "My dear fox, go and fetch me some of the meat which the King is to eat today."

The fox was more cunning than the hare, and went through the lanes and alleys, without seeing a dog, straight to the royal palace, and into the room where the Princess was, under whose stool he crept. Presently he scratched her foot, and the Princess, looking down, recognized the fox with her necklace, and, taking him into her room, she asked, "What do you want, dear fox?" He replied,

"My master who killed the dragon is here and sent me to beg a piece of the meat such as the King will eat today."

The Princess summoned the cook and made her prepare a dish of meat like the King's and, when it was ready, carry it for the fox to the door of the inn. Then the fox took the dish himself and, first driving the flies away with a whisk of his tail, carried it in to the hunter.

"See here, Master Landlord," said the hunter, "here are the bread and meat. Now I will have the same vegetables as the King eats."

He called the wolf and said, "Dear wolf, go and fetch me some vegetables the same as the King eats today."

The wolf went straight to the castle like a person who feared nobody, and when he came to the Princess, he plucked at her clothes so that she looked around. The maiden knew the wolf by his necklace and took him with her into her room and said, "Dear wolf, what do you want?"

The beast replied, "My master who killed the dragon is here and has sent me for some vegetables like those the King eats today."

Then she bade the cook prepare a dish of vegetables the same as the King's, and carry it to the inn door for the wolf, who took it from her and bore it in to his master. The hunter said, "See here, my host, now I have bread, meat, and vegetables the same as the King's, but I will also have the same sweetmeats." Then he called to the bear, "Dear bear, go and fetch me some sweetmeats like those the King has for his dinner today, for you like sweet things." The bear rolled along up to the castle, while everyone got out of his way, but, when he came to the guard, the guard pointed his gun at him and would not let him pass into the royal apartments. The bear, however, got up on his hind legs and boxed the guard right and left on the ears with his paw, which knocked him down; thereupon he went straight to the room where the Princess was, and, getting behind her, growled slightly. She looked around and perceived the bear, whom she took into her own chamber and asked what he had come for. "My master who slew the dragon is here," said he, "and has sent me for some sweetmeats such as the King eats." The Princess let the pastry cook be called and bade him prepare sweetmeats like those the King had and carry them for the bear to the inn. There the bear took charge of them, and, first licking off the sugar that had boiled over, he took them in to his master.

"See here, friend landlord," said the huntsman, "now I have bread, meat, vegetables, and sweetmeats from the table of the King, but I mean also to drink his wine."

He called the lion and said, "Dear lion, I should bc glad to have a draft. Go and fetch me some wine like that which the King drinks."

The lion strode through the town, where all the people made way for him, and soon came to the castle, where the watchmen attempted to stop him at the gates, but just by giving a little bit of a roar, he frightened them so that they all ran away. He walked on to the royal apartments and knocked with his tail on the door. When the Princess opened it, she was at first frightened to see a lion, but, soon recognizing him by the gold clasp of her necklace which he wore, she took him into her room and asked, "Dear lion, what do you wish?"

The lion replied, "My master who killed the dragon is here and has sent me to fetch him wine like that which the King drinks at his own table." The Princess summoned the butler and told him to give the lion wine such as the King drank. But the lion said, "I will go down with you and see that I have the right wine." So he went with the butler, who was about to draw the ordinary wine, such as was drunk by the King's servants, but the lion cried, "Wait! I will first taste the wine," and, drawing for himself half a cupful, he drank it and said, "No! That is not the real wine." The butler looked at him askance and went to draw from another cask which was made for the King's Marshal. Then the lion cried, "Wait! First

I must taste it." He drew half a flagonful and drank it and said, "This is better, but it is still not the right wine." At these words the butler got into a rage and said, "What does such a stupid fool as you know about wine?" The lion gave him a blow behind the ear, so that he fell down, and as soon as he came to himself he quite submissively led the lion into a little cellar where the King's wine was kept, which no one ever dared to taste. But the lion drew for himself half a cupful and tried the wine and said, "This must be the real stuff," and bade the butler fill six bottles with it. When this was done, they mounted the steps again, and as the lion came out of the cellar into the fresh air he reeled about, being a little tipsy, so that the butler had to carry the wine basket for him to the inn, where the lion, taking it again in his mouth, carried it in to his master. The hunter called the landlord, and said, "See here, now I have bread, meat, vegetables, sweetmeats, and wine, the very same as the King will himself eat today, and so I will have my dinner with my animals." They sat down and ate and drank, for he gave the hare, the fox, the wolf, the bear, and the lion their share of the good things, and he was very happy, for he felt the King's daughter still loved him. When he had finished his meal he said to the landlord, "Now, as I have eaten and drunk the same things as the King, I will go to the royal palace and marry the Princess."

The landlord said, "How can that be, for she is already betrothed, and today the wedding is to be celebrated!"

Then the hunter drew out the handkerchief which the King's daughter had given him on the dragon's mountain, and in which the seven tongues of the dragon's seven heads were wrapped, and said, "This will help me to do it."

The landlord looked at the handkerchief and said, "Even if I believe everything that has been done, still I cannot believe that, and I will wager my house and garden on it."

Thereupon the huntsman took out a purse with a thousand gold pieces in it, and said, "I will bet you that against your house and garden."

Meantime the King asked his daughter, "What is the meaning of all these wild beasts which have come to you today and passed and repassed in and out of my castle?"

She replied, "I dare not tell you, but let the master of these beasts be fetched, and you will do well."

The King sent a servant to the inn to invite the strange man to come. The servant arrived at the inn just as the hunter had concluded his wager with the landlord. So the hunter said, "See, my host, the King even sends a servant to invite me to come, but I am not going yet." And to the servant he said, "I beg the King to send me royal clothes and a carriage with six horses and servants to wait on me."

When the King heard this answer, he said to his daughter, "What shall I do?" "Do as he desires, and you will do well," she replied. So the King sent a suit of royal clothes, a carriage with six horses, and some servants to wait on the man. When the hunter saw them coming, he said to the landlord, "See here, I am getting everything I desired," and he put on the royal clothes, took the handkerchief with him, and drove to the King. When the King saw the huntsman coming, he asked his daughter how he should receive him, and she said, "Go out to meet him, and you will do well." So the King met the huntsman and led him into the palace, the animals following. The King showed him a seat near himself and his daughter, and the Marshal sat upon the other side as the bridegroom. Now, against the wall was placed the seven-headed dragon, stuffed as if it were still alive, and the King said, "The seven heads of that dragon were cut off by our Marshal, to whom this day I give my daughter in marriage."

Then the hunter rose and, opening the seven jaws of the dragon, asked where were the seven tongues. This frightened the Marshal, and he turned pale as death, but at last, not knowing what else to say, he stammered out, "Dragons have no tongues."

The hunter replied, "*Liars* should have none, but the dragon's tongues are the trophies of the dragon slayer," and, so saying, he unwrapped the handkerchief, and there lay all seven, and he put one into each mouth of the monster, and they fitted exactly. Then he took the handkerchief on which her name was embroidered and showed it to the maiden and asked her to whom she had given it, and she replied, "To him who slew the dragon." Then he called his beasts, and taking from each the necklace, and from the lion the golden clasp, he put them together. He showed them to the Princess and asked to whom they belonged. The Princess said, "The necklace and the clasp were mine, and I shared it among the animals who helped to conquer the dragon." Then the huntsman said, "When I was weary and rested after the fight, the Marshal came and cut off my head, and then took the Princess away and said that it was he who had conquered the dragon. Now that he has lied, I show these tongues, this necklace, and this handkerchief as proof." And then he related how the beasts had cured him with a wonderful root, and that for a year he had wandered and at last had come here again, where he had discovered the deceit of the Marshal through the inn-keeper's tale. Then the King asked his daughter, "Is it true that this man killed the dragon?"

"Yes," she replied, "it is true, for I dared not disclose the treachery of the Marshal, because he threatened me with instant death. But now it is known without my revealing it, and for this reason I delayed the wedding a year and a day."

After these words the King ordered twelve councillors summoned who would judge the Marshal, and these condemned him to be torn to pieces by four oxen. So the Marshal was executed, and the King gave his daughter to the huntsman and named him ruler over all his kingdom. The wedding was celebrated with great joy, and the young King caused his father and foster father to be brought to him and loaded them with presents. He did not forget the landlord, but bade him welcome, and said to him, "See here, my host, I have married the daughter of the King, and your house and garden are mine." The landlord said that was according to right, but the young King said, "It shall be according to mercy," and he not only gave him back his house and garden but presented him with the thousand gold pieces he had wagered.

Now the young King and Queen were very happy and lived together in contentment. He often went out hunting, because he delighted in it, and the faithful animals always accompanied him.

In the neighborhood there was a forest which, it was said, was haunted. It was also said that if one entered it, he would not easily get out again. The young King, however, had a great desire to hunt in it, and he let the old King have no peace till he consented. The young King then rode away with a great company, and, as he approached the forest, he saw a snow-white hind going into it. Telling his companions to await his return, he rode off among the trees, and only his faithful beasts accompanied him. The courtiers waited and waited till evening, but he did not return, so they rode home and told the young Queen that her husband had ridden into the forest after a white doe and had not come out again. The news made her very anxious about him. He, however, had ridden farther and farther into the wood after the beautiful animal without catching it; when he thought it was within range of his gun, with one spring it got away, till at last it disappeared altogether. Then he realized for the first time how deeply he had plunged into the thickets. He gave a blast on his horn, but there was no answer, for his people could not hear it. Presently night began to close in. Realizing that he could not get home that day, he dismounted, made a fire, and prepared to pass the night. While he sat by the fire, with his beasts lying all around him, he thought he heard a human voice, but when he looked around, he could see nobody. Soon after he heard a groan, as if from a box, and, looking up, he saw an old woman sitting in the tree. She was groaning and crying, "Oh, oh, oh, how frozen I am!" He called out, "Come down and warm yourself if you're freezing." But she said, "No, your beasts will bite me." He replied, "They will not harm you, my good lady, if you'd like to come down." But she was a witch and said, "I will throw you down a twig—if you beat them on their backs with it, they then will do nothing to me." He did as she requested, and immediately the animals lay down quietly enough, for they were changed into stone. Now that the old woman was safe from the animals, she sprang down, and, touching the King, too, with a twig, she changed him into stone. Thereupon she laughed to herself and buried him and his beasts in a grave, where there were many more stones.

Meantime the young Queen was becoming more and more anxious and sad because her husband did not return. Just then it happened that the other brother, who had traveled toward the east when they separated, came into the territory. He had been seeking and had found no service to enter, and was, therefore, traveling through the country and making his animals dance for a living. Once he thought he would go and look at the knife which they had stuck in a tree when they separated, so he could see how his brother fared. When he looked at it, lo! his brother's side was half rusty and half bright! At this he was frightened and thought his brother must have fallen into some great misfortune, but he hoped to save him, for half the knife was bright. He therefore went with his beasts toward the west, and as he came to the capital city, the watchman went out to meet him and asked if he should mention his arrival to his bride, for the young Queen had for two days been in great sorrow and distress at his absence and feared he had been killed in the enchanted wood. The watchman thought certainly he was no one else but the young King, for he was so much like him and also had the same wild beasts returning with him. The huntsman perceived that the watchman was speaking of his brother, and he thought it would be all for the best for him to pass as his brother, for by so doing he might more easily save him. So he let himself be conducted by the watchman into the castle and was there received with great joy, for the young Queen took him for her husband also, and asked him where he had been so long. He told her he had lost his way in a wood and had been unable to find his way out earlier.

For a couple of days he rested at home, but he was always asking about the enchanted wood, and at last he said, "I must hunt there once more." The King and the young Queen tried to dissuade him, but he was determined and went out with a great number of attendants. As soon as he got into the wood, the same thing happened to him as had happened to his brother: he saw a white hind and told his people to wait for him while he hunted the wild animal, and he immediately rode off, with his beasts following him. But he could not catch the hind any more than his brother had, and he went so deep into the wood that he had to spend the night there. As soon as he had made a fire, he heard someone groaning above him, and saying, "Oh, oh, oh, how frozen I am!" Then he looked up, and there sat the same old witch in the tree, and he said to her, "If you're freezing, old woman, why don't you come down and warm yourself?" She replied, "No, your beasts would bite me, but if you would beat them with a twig I'd throw down to you, they could do me no harm." When the hunter heard this, he doubted the old woman and said to her, "I do not beat my beasts, so come down, or I will fetch you." But she called out, "What are you thinking of? You can do nothing to me." He answered, "Come down, or I will shoot you." The old woman laughed and said, "Shoot away! I am not afraid of your bullets!"

He knelt down and shot, but she was bulletproof, and laughing till she yelled, she called out, "You can't catch me!" However, the hunter knew a trick or two. He tore three silver buttons from his coat and loaded his gun with them. While he was ramming them down, the old witch threw herself out of the tree with a loud shriek, for she was not proof against such shot. He placed his foot on her neck and said, "Old witch, if you do not tell me quickly where my brother is, I will tie your hands together and throw you into the fire!"

She was in great anguish and begged for mercy and said, "He lies with his beasts in a grave, turned into stone." Then he forced her to go with him, threatening her, and saying, "You old cat! Now turn my brother and all the creatures lying here into their proper forms, or I will throw you into the fire!"

The old witch took a twig and changed the stones back to what they were, and immediately his brother and the beasts stood before the huntsman, as well as many merchants, workmen, and shepherds who, delighted with their freedom, returned home. The twin brothers, when they saw each other again, kissed and embraced, and were very glad. They seized the old witch, bound her, and laid her on the fire, and when she was consumed, the forest itself disappeared, and all was clear and free, so that one could see the royal palace three miles off.

Now the two brothers went home together and on the way told each other their adventures. And when the one said he was lord over the whole land in place of the King, the other one said, "I was well aware of all that, for when I went into the city I was taken for you. And all kingly honor was paid to me, the young Queen even mistaking me for her true husband and making me sit at her table and sleep in her room." When the first one heard this, he became so angry and so jealous that he drew his sword and cut off the head of his brother. But as soon as he had done so and saw the red blood flowing from the dead body, he repented sorely and said, "My brother has saved me, and I have killed him for so doing," and he groaned pitifully. Just then the hare came and offered to fetch the healing root. He ran off and brought it just at the right time, so that the dead man was restored to life again, and not even the mark of the wound was to be seen.

After this adventure they went on, and the first brother said, "You see that we both have on royal robes, and both have the same beasts following us. We will, therefore, enter the city at opposite gates and arrive from the two quarters at the same time before the King."

So they separated, and at the same moment the watchman from each gate came to the King and informed him that the young King with the beasts had returned from the hunt. The King said, "It is not possible, for your two gates are a mile apart!" But in the meantime the two brothers had arrived in the castle yard, and began to mount the stairs. When they entered, the King said to his daughter, "Tell me which is your husband, for one appears to me the same as the other, and I cannot tell." The Princess was in great trouble, and could not tell which was which, but at last she thought of the necklace she had given to the beasts, and she looked and found on one of the lions her golden clasp, and then she cried exultingly, "He to whom this lion belongs is my rightful husband." Then the young King laughed and said, "Yes, that is right," and they sat down together at table and ate and drank and were merry. At night when the young King went to bed, his wife asked him why he had placed on the two previous nights a sword in the bed, for she thought it was to kill her. Then the young King knew how faithful his brother had been.